She shook her head emphatically. "This isn't a marriage proposal. It's a stunt, a PR exercise."

"That's what's bothering you?" Raif leaned closer, capturing her other hand where it was pressed against her collarbone. He kissed one, then the other, inhaling her rose and cinnamon scent. "Tara Michaels, would you do me the inestimable honor of marrying me?"

Instead of melting at his words, she stiffened. Tara shot to her feet, pulling free and stumbling toward the window before swinging back to face him, eyes wounded. "That's not funny."

"I wasn't aiming for humor." Raif stood, pride stiffening his spine.

"You're seriously talking about marriage?"

Did she think he made a habit of proposing? Never had Raif offered marriage. Never had he thought about spending the rest of his life with any woman, though he'd known it was his duty to marry one day to secure the throne.

"Deadly serious."

Once more she shook her head. He reminded himself the circumstances were extraordinary.

"Why should I marry you? I barely know you."

Growing up near the beach, **Annie West** spent lots of time observing tall, burnished lifeguards—early research! Now she spends her days fantasizing about gorgeous men and their love lives. Annie has been a reader all her life. She also loves travel, long walks, good company and great food. You can contact her at annie@annie-west.com or via PO Box 1041, Warners Bay, NSW 2282, Australia.

Books by Annie West

Harlequin Presents

Demanding His Desert Queen
Contracted to Her Greek Enemy
Claiming His Out-of-Bounds Bride

Passion in Paradise

Wedding Night Reunion in Greece

Secret Heirs of Billionaires

Sheikh's Royal Baby Revelation

Sovereigns and Scandals

Revelations of a Secret Princess
The King's Bride by Arrangement

Visit the Author Profile page
at Harlequin.com for more titles.

Annie West

THE SHEIKH'S MARRIAGE PROCLAMATION

HARLEQUIN
PRESENTS

HARLEQUIN®
PRESENTS®

Recycling programs for this product may not exist in your area.

ISBN-13: 978-1-335-40394-0

The Sheikh's Marriage Proclamation

Copyright © 2021 by Annie West

This edition published by arrangement with Harlequin Books S.A.

For questions and comments about the quality of this book, please contact us at CustomerService@Harlequin.com.

Harlequin Enterprises ULC
22 Adelaide St. West, 40th Floor
Toronto, Ontario M5H 4E3, Canada
www.Harlequin.com

Printed in U.S.A.

THE SHEIKH'S MARRIAGE PROCLAMATION

This one is for Erica Venning.

Thanks for being so positive and enthusiastic!

CHAPTER ONE

THE TRUCK STOPPED and Tara's pulse quickened. This was the part she feared. The dangerous part.

She could barely believe she was doing this, breaking the law, trying to enter a country illegally.

Escaping a country. That was more to the point.

She shuddered, thinking of her fate if she stayed in Dhalkur.

Any qualms about putting herself into the hands of a man she barely knew in order to escape faded compared to that.

The alternative, to remain in her mother's country, at Fuad's mercy, was impossible. Nausea swirled through her stomach and the stifling heat made her skin prickle.

Fear clawed at her. It made her ribs contract around her lungs and shortened her breath. Though perhaps the latter was also because of her tight cocoon, wedged in the back of the truck. It was early but the desert heat was rising.

There was a jolt, as if the driver climbed down or someone climbed aboard. Then the engine started and they rolled forward.

They'd passed the border.

Relief seared Tara's lungs as she sucked in a great

gulp of air. As much as she could, anyway. There was precious little space and very little air, but she couldn't let herself think of that. She couldn't get claustrophobic now. Yunis would stop the truck once they were out of sight of the border and help her out of this confined space. All she had to do was keep calm and wait.

That took everything she had. The last month had been the worst of her life and now it had turned into a nightmare. Grief still ate away at her, making the world seem dull and grey. Everything except Fuad. *Him* she saw in Technicolor. And wished she didn't.

She never wanted to see him again. Her cousin had grown from a spiteful, sadistic boy into a ruthless, grasping man, ready to flatten anyone who stood between him and what he wanted.

Like Tara.

She shivered again, telling herself that soon she'd be free. The truck would stop and Yunis would let her out. Yunis, who'd known her mother years before and who took this enormous risk to help Tara. When she was safely away she'd find a way to repay him.

Tara yawned, tired despite the danger. Heat and lack of oxygen took their toll.

Soon they'd stop, and when they did…

She woke to panic and darkness. Heat pressed down on her, stifling. She couldn't move, her arms and legs were trapped. She couldn't see. She couldn't hear either. It was as if she were bound and weighted. Totally disorientated, she couldn't even tell which way was up.

Tara was about to scream when memory hit. The truck. The border. Yunis's offer to hide her in a delivery of merchandise he was taking into Nahrat.

She'd fallen asleep, that was all. She almost sobbed her relief.

Had she been this unbearably hot before? In the close darkness her overheated skin itched and her hair clung damply. How long had she been here?

There was a resonant thump as the back of the truck opened. Were those voices?

Instantly she closed her mouth on the words forming on her lips. Yunis was heading to the capital of Nahrat but promised to set her down somewhere quiet. The plan didn't involve other people.

Yet there they were again, male voices, muffled because of the way she was concealed and by the blood beating in her ears.

Where were they? Who were they? Had she made a mistake trusting the man who'd been her mother's friend?

Heart in mouth, she felt movement. Someone tugged at the bundle that concealed her. Masculine voices and a huff of laughter, and then, with a lurching sway that made her glad she'd had no time for breakfast, she was upended over something that might have been a shoulder.

Tara bit her lip, tasting blood, as she suppressed a cry of shock and discomfort. Fully awake now, unable to move, all she could do was stay silent and hope the change of plan didn't mean Fuad had found her.

Acid bit her belly at the idea of facing Fuad again.

Or the possibility of Yunis delivering her somewhere else. To ruthless men who'd have a use for Fuad's female cousin that she didn't want to think about.

Raif waited till he was alone then rose from the gilded seat at the centre of the marble dais. He stretched mightily, lifting his shoulders to ease the kinks there.

Despite his discomfort, his weekly public hearing of appeals was one centuries-old tradition he had no intention of changing. It was important people felt they had the ear of their Sheikh.

Today's session had started with a land dispute that had simmered for several generations, and which would try the wisdom of Solomon. From there he'd heard of an alleged dowry theft, issues with planning and electoral zone changes, and an accusation of impropriety against a government official.

Raif was particularly concerned by the allegation against the official. He administered funds for community-based projects and if true—

The doors opened and the palace chamberlain entered, bowing. He gestured to a tall man who carried something long over his shoulder. Even from here Raif saw the stranger was sweating, his breathing heavy and his eyes wide. Was his burden so heavy or was he nervous? The royal audience chamber was designed to impress visitors with its regal opulence.

'Quickly.' The chamberlain chivvied the man. 'Don't keep His Majesty waiting.'

Another bow and the chamberlain approached the royal dais. 'Sir, you asked to be informed when the gift for your aunt arrived.' He gestured towards the man slowly making his way across the floor of intricately inlaid stone. 'One of my staff happened to be at the border when the shipment came through, and ensured it was brought here immediately. I thought you'd want to view it to ensure it meets with your approval.'

Raif nodded. His chamberlain was a good man but sometimes too officious, eager to micromanage. He wouldn't be surprised if the palace official who'd happened to be at the border had been ordered to wait for the shipment. As if the delivery needed a special escort!

He transferred his attention to the stranger, who, with a huff of effort, carefully placed his burden on the floor. Then he bowed, keeping his head low.

'You may rise.'

Even then the newcomer seemed reluctant, straightening but staring in the direction of Raif's feet.

'Open the wrapping, so His Majesty can see.' The chamberlain stepped towards the package but instantly the stranger intercepted the movement, as if guarding his consignment.

'No!' He turned and for the first time met Raif's eyes. The skin drew tight at the back of Raif's neck. That look spoke of urgency, desperation even. 'If it pleases Your Majesty. You need to see this in private.' He looked over his shoulder towards the guard on the door.

Curious, Raif surveyed the stranger. 'Why is that?'

The man's mouth worked as if trying out and rejecting several responses. His hands twisted together. 'Please, Your Majesty. It's important. This is only for your eyes.'

Even the chamberlain looked surprised. 'Come now.' He started forward, as if to take matters into his own hands, but once more the stranger blocked the attempt.

'And you are?' Raif's voice cut across their altercation.

'Yunis, Your Majesty. I'm head of the Dhalkuri Royal Guild of—'

'I know who you are.' His aunt had sung this man's praises, which was why Raif had commissioned this gift for her from his workshop. 'I look forward to seeing what you've brought.'

Not merely because he wanted something special for his aunt, but because Raif's interest was piqued. His aunt hadn't only praised his work, but also his character.

'Please, Your Majesty.' Another, lingering look over his shoulder then Yunis placed a hand on his heart. 'I swear I mean no harm.'

Curiouser and curiouser. With an abrupt nod Raif dismissed the guard, who stepped out and closed the door behind him.

'Your Majesty!' the chamberlain expostulated.

Raif ignored him. Yunis wouldn't have been able to enter the palace if armed. Besides, Raif's aunt had vouched for him.

'Open it,' he ordered.

Yunis shot the chamberlain a last, disapproving stare then knelt and untied the strips of fabric binding the cylinder. He murmured something beneath his breath that Raif couldn't catch, then slowly, as carefully as if it were made of spun gold threaded with precious jewels, he unwrapped the parcel.

A tasselled edge of pale gold caught the light, as if giving flesh to Raif's imaginings. Now Yunis unrolled more, shuffling further away as the long carpet was revealed. Golds mixed with the pale colours of the desert sands, contrasting with indigo blues and deep purples.

His aunt would love it. The colours were her favourites and not usually chosen by traditional weavers. Raif could see the piece was beautifully made. Yet why the demand for privacy? Why take so long to unroll it?

The chamberlain obviously thought the same thing.

Before Yunis could stop him he grabbed one side and yanked. The carpet unspooled with a thud and an unexpected flurry and Raif found himself staring down at bare limbs, a tangle of dark hair and huge, staring eyes.

The chamberlain jumped back, exclaiming. Yunis froze.

And still Raif stared.

She, for it was undoubtedly a she, wore a dress the colour of ripe raspberries. Or half wore it, for there seemed to be a lot of glowing golden flesh on display. Shapely calves and smooth thighs. Her breasts rose and fell beneath their scant crimson covering as she sucked in huge gasps of air. And still those eyes stared back at him.

Raif felt the impact of that stare somewhere near the base of his spine and deeper, in his gut.

Finally, a slender arm lifted and she pushed back the swathe of long hair to reveal a flushed face.

She was beautiful, or close to it.

Perhaps it was the ripe mouth that made her look so ravishing. She had full lips, slightly downturned at the corners. That should have made her appear disgruntled but instead created a sultry look.

Raif felt another phantom jab to his belly.

The flush mantling her cheeks, throat and the upper slopes of her breasts, the tumble of dark hair and her breathlessness inevitably made Raif think of bed. Of bed and passion.

'Cleopatra, I presume?'

The voice suited him. It trawled dark, deep and dangerous through her middle, like a velvet ribbon wound around metal.

For there was definitely steel in that voice. She saw
it too in those hooded eyes, hawk-like in their intensity.
In the arrogant angle of his jaw and the black eyebrow
that snaked up his forehead in an expression of enquiry
mixed with derision.

Already tall, he towered above her from a raised
platform, making her feel tiny and insignificant,
sprawled before him. His formal robes, pristine white
and trimmed with gold, contrasted with her bedrag-
gled state. His folded arms spoke of authority tinged
with impatience.

He was magnificent.

And he knew it.

Feminine instinct, old as the ages, told her this man
understood the aura of power and unadulterated mas-
culinity he projected. Knew and revelled in it.

Or simply took it for granted.

Blinking, still catching her breath, half dazed from
discomfort and lack of oxygen, she took too long to
understand the Cleopatra reference. Then it struck her.
Cleopatra supposedly had herself smuggled into Julius
Caesar's quarters wrapped in a carpet, then famously
proceeded to seduce him.

Shock stabbed her, and a rising tide of mortification.

Tara groped with unsteady fingers at the tie of her
wraparound dress, only to discover the bow undone
and the dress gaping.

With a gasp of horror she fumbled, searching for
the loose ends, hampered by hands that were too slow
and a heaving stomach that threatened to embarrass
her totally.

She heard voices, Yunis's perhaps, but couldn't take
them in, overcome by the twin needs to cover her body

and stop herself from retching. The long journey, stifling and overheated, left her prey to welling nausea.

Beyond the fringe of the carpet she saw intricate designs of semi-precious stones set into the marble floor. She lifted her head again and had an impression of enormous space. A domed, glittering ceiling above a room empty but for the podium where *he* stood.

The setting confirmed her fears. In that first instant facing him she'd been too befuddled and sick to do more than drink in his presence. Now the truth smacked her in the face.

This was no ordinary room. As the man surveying her so imperiously was no ordinary man.

Tara knew that austere, handsome face. Anyone with an interest in current affairs would recognise it.

Yunis hadn't sold her to some human trafficker. He'd brought her to the Sheikh of Nahrat.

Appalled, she felt her rebellious stomach lurch and her skin prickle.

She'd made it over the border but she wasn't safe. Bad enough to be discovered as an illegal alien sneaking into his country. But that would be nothing compared with her fate if he discovered who she was and decided to return her to her cousin.

Sick to the depths of her curdling stomach, Tara grasped her dress tight around herself and tottered to her feet, pushing her shoulders back and setting her jaw.

'Your Majesty.' She couldn't manage a curtsey, much less a bow, so she simply dipped her head and focused on staying upright despite the wobbling knees and whirling nausea.

'That was quite a performance.'

Impossible to gauge his mood from his words. Was he being sarcastic? She didn't lift her head to find out. Instead Tara swallowed hard, telling herself she would not be ill. She would *not*!

'Your name?'

Slowly she raised her eyes, hoping that this time he wouldn't look quite so indomitable. Tara wasn't sure she had the energy to deal with indomitable at the moment.

It was a vain hope. Sheikh Raif ibn Ansar of Nahrat looked more unmovable and keen-eyed than before.

'Tara, Your Majesty.' She drew a deep breath and mentally crossed her fingers. It was unlikely her surname would mean anything to him. 'Tara Michaels.'

'And the meaning of this exhibition, Ms Michaels?' His eyes narrowed on her. 'I admit it's a novel entrance but it lacks…dignity.' He didn't appear to move yet suddenly he looked even more imposing. 'Despite what some believe, I have no interest in women falling at my feet, literally or otherwise.'

His stare didn't leave her face but that didn't stop her searing blush, as if he'd raked that sharp gaze across her whole body.

Because something about his scrutiny made her inescapably aware of herself as a woman and him as a man.

Or because he'd already looked and found her wanting?

Then there was his outrageous assumption she'd *planned* this humiliating scene.

As if any sane woman would have herself unrolled at his feet like some…offering! She'd bet that old story about Cleopatra had been invented by a man. A man with a salacious mind.

Indignation sputtered to life.

'If you please, Your Majesty.' Yunis stepped forward to stand beside her. 'It was a mistake. This wasn't meant to happen.' He turned to Tara, his weathered features creased with worry. 'I was met at the border. I had no chance to stop and let you out before reaching the palace.'

'People smuggling,' said another voice, and a rotund little man moved into Tara's line of vision. 'I'll call the guard and have them locked up.'

At the words, Tara's strength crumbled. The thought of being locked up again, on top of what she'd been through! Her knees folded but Yunis grabbed her elbow, holding her steady.

'There's no need for that,' said the Sheikh. 'I'll interview them myself. You may go. And you will keep this to yourself until I decide what action to take.'

Tara barely heard the little man leave. But she did hear the firm tread of the Sheikh's feet as he stepped from the dais and crossed the floor.

'Are you ill?'

Tara struggled to straighten her spine and lock her knees. 'Motion sickness,' she muttered. 'There was no air in there and it got so hot.'

For long, silent seconds the Sheikh regarded her. He was close enough for her to see that his eyes were so dark they seemed black. The effect was arresting.

The need to meet his scrutiny, not to waver or look away, helped her fight her uneasy stomach and shaky limbs.

'Come,' he said finally. He turned and left the room, not bothering to see if they followed.

Twenty minutes later, Tara sat in a luxuriously appointed sitting room. Her chair was so comfortable she wanted to curl up in it and rest her weary head. She hadn't slept last night and the day had been fraught.

She'd half expected to be led to a bare interrogation cell. Instead, a smiling woman had brought a jug of iced water and a plate of biscuits.

Now Tara's nausea had receded, all she wanted was to leave. Except the Sheikh had taken Yunis with him and Tara couldn't leave without making sure Yunis was okay. It was her fault he was in this mess.

She would have searched for him except for the guard standing to attention outside the room.

So she contented herself with resting her head against the soft upholstery and closing her eyes, recruiting her strength.

She wasn't sure what woke her. Not a sound, but perhaps the sensation of being watched.

Tara opened her eyes and discovered she wasn't alone.

Fathomless dark eyes surveyed her. Sheikh Raif of Nahrat didn't even blink as he sat there, watching her.

Hurriedly Tara unfolded her legs, which had been tucked up beneath her, and sat straighter, feet to the floor. Tentatively she felt with her toes for her discarded sandals then gave up. So she was barefoot. He'd already seen her with her dress half undone. What were bare feet after that?

Swiftly checking the neckline of her dress hadn't

gaped as she slept, Tara folded her hands primly in her lap. 'Where's Yunis?'

'You don't need to worry about him.'

'I don't?' Her head seemed thick and slow to work. 'You've released him? He's free?'

The Sheikh tapped the fingers of one hand on the arm of his chair. 'Of course not. He broke the law, smuggling you over the border. The rest of his consignment is being examined. Who knows what else he's smuggled in?'

Tara shook her head. 'It's not like that. He's not really a smuggler.'

'Not *really*?' He looked sceptical.

'It's *true*! He brought me in as a favour.'

'That's hardly an excuse for people smuggling. It's a serious offence. If he has no respect for our borders he may have committed other offences too. He'll be treated accordingly.'

The Sheikh looked so severe that Tara's heart dipped. She sat forward onto the edge of her seat, hands clasped.

'What have you done with him?'

Nahrat was reputedly a progressive country with modern laws. But recent contact with Fuad had proved how little the law meant when a powerful, merciless man chose to ignore it. Was Yunis facing more than interrogation? Horrified, she shot to her feet.

'Have you hurt him?'

The Sheikh sat back in his seat. 'Would it matter if I had?'

Horror crawled up Tara's spine and filled her mouth. She felt the blood drain to her toes.

'Of course it matters! Torture is wrong, as well as illegal.'

She dragged in a shaky breath but kept her gaze fixed on that enigmatic stare. She'd thought those dark eyes sexy. Now they seemed full of threat. 'Truly, he's a decent man. He's never done this before. He saw I was desperate and offered me a chance to escape. He was trying to help.'

The Sheikh nodded. 'So he says. He's currently waiting, unharmed, while his story is verified.'

Tara felt herself deflate like a punctured balloon. She landed back on the chair with a thump, her pounding heart at odds with her suddenly boneless body.

'Why did you let me think you'd hurt him?'

'That was purely your imagination, Ms Michaels. And a very vivid one it is.' He paused, and when he spoke again it was with the harsh ring of authority. Or was it annoyance? 'I uphold the law in my country, which means even wrongdoers receive a fair hearing.'

Tara noted the frown lines creasing his forehead and the now flat line of his mouth.

Had she bruised his pride with her question? Surely not. He'd deliberately toyed with her, making her worry. To unsettle her?

She'd spent too much time recently with Fuad. Her cousin stopped at nothing to get what he wanted and didn't shy from causing pain. In fact, he seemed to thrive on it. Had she wrongly tarred the Sheikh with the same brush?

'Tell me the truth, Ms Michaels.'

'I am!' Sitting straight, she fixed him with what she hoped was a calm look, when inside she felt anything but calm.

She'd escaped Fuad's clutches but if this man sent her back across the border there'd be no second chance to escape. She couldn't afford to go back. The question was, how much could she share with this man? How much could she trust him?

'I'm a British citizen and—'

'Congratulations. You speak our language well.'

'I…' How much to reveal? 'My mother was from Dhalkur and I was born there. I lived there till I was eight.'

'And you've come back to visit your family?'

Tara hesitated. This was unsafe territory. If he discovered who her cousin was, he'd feel obliged to return her.

'My mother is dead, Your Majesty.' Her throat turned scratchy and she found herself swallowing convulsively. A month wasn't long enough to adjust to the loss.

She looked down at her hands, saw them clenched, bone-white with tension, and made them relax. When she looked up the Sheikh's gaze was unreadable.

'There was nothing to keep me in Dhalkur. I want to go home. But I…lost my passport—'

'And your luggage?'

'Sorry?'

'My staff inform me no baggage was found in the truck. You were travelling light, Ms Michaels.'

Because if she'd been seen walking down into the courtyard with a suitcase she'd most definitely have been stopped. But she couldn't say that.

Tara forced herself to shrug. 'I was in a hurry. I have to get back to London quickly and Yunis offered to help me. He's an old friend of my mother's, from years ago.' That much was true, at least.

'So, instead of going to the authorities and reporting the loss of your passport, you chose to break the law, and incite your accomplice to do the same, by crossing the border illegally.'

His face was calm but his voice was stern, like a judge pronouncing sentence.

'Surely you can do better than that, Ms Michaels.' His mouth lifted at one corner in a cold smile that made her shiver. 'Or should I call you Princess Tara?'

CHAPTER TWO

TARA'S BREATH ESCAPED in a whoosh of defeat. Her shoulders sagged and she slumped back against the sumptuous upholstery.

This was it, then. No chance to escape now.

Despair cut through her. A chill blast of fear iced her bones at the idea of going back. She shivered and would have crossed her arms against the sudden cold except this eagle-eyed man would notice.

He noticed everything, she was sure.

There was no surprise on his features, not even satisfaction that he'd guessed right.

'You knew! All this time you knew and you didn't say anything.' That stiffened her backbone.

He shrugged, his wide shoulders rising with nonchalant ease. 'I was waiting for you to tell me.'

As if she had any reason to trust him. For all she knew he was a friend of Fuad's.

'*Is* Yunis okay? Will you release him now you have me?'

Something changed in that hard, handsome face. For a second it looked as if she'd surprised him. Yet how could that be? He was the one who'd walked into the room knowing her identity.

'You make it sound as if I *want* to have you.'

Tara blinked. Was there a chance he'd simply let her go? But she was clutching at straws. Even if he wasn't a friend of her cousin's, as leader of a neighbouring country he'd feel obliged to return her to Fuad. He wouldn't want to fracture relations for the sake of a woman he didn't even know.

'Please, at least let him go. Yunis was trying to do a good deed, that's all.'

'Yunis again?' This time his frown was more than a slight twitch across his forehead. 'Does he mean that much to you? What is he? A lover?'

'Of course not!' How had he made that leap? 'He's old enough to be my father!' She met the Sheikh's sceptical gaze and shook her head. 'He's an old friend of my mother's,' she reiterated. 'They knew each other before she married. He helped me for her sake.'

For long seconds there was silence, then finally he inclined his head. 'Fortunately, your Yunis is also a trusted acquaintance of my aunt. After questioning him it was obvious he's not in the habit of smuggling. He'll be released with a warning.'

Tara's heart thundered with relief. It was enough, almost, to counteract indignation at the way this man had manipulated her. 'Thank you. He's a good man. I'd hate to see him punished for this.'

She'd bear punishment enough for two when she was taken back across the border.

'Is it possible, do you think...? Could you *not* mention his name when you talk to the authorities in Dhalkur?' Because even if the Sheikh of Nahrat refused to press charges, Fuad would make Yunis pay and his methods were likely to be ones Tara preferred not to think about.

'I'll consider it.' He paused. 'Depending on how straight you are with me, Princess.'

Tara stiffened. 'Don't. Please. I'm not a princess.'

Ebony eyebrows rose. 'You're the niece of the ruling Sheikh of Dhalkur.'

Tara hiked her chin up. 'But I'm not royal. I wasn't raised in the palace and I can't inherit the throne. My father was British.' The law in Dhalkur decreed that only men could lead the nation. Just as well. She couldn't imagine herself in that role.

'Yet some would say your lineage is more royal than your cousin Fuad's.'

Something inside her stalled. Was it possible Fuad, and by extension this man, saw her as a threat to Fuad's rule?

Her neck tingled with a presentiment of fear. She'd thought her fate bad enough, when trapped in Dhalkur, but if Fuad saw her as a rival, rather than a convenient tool to be exploited...

'Fuad is my uncle's eldest son. When my uncle dies Fuad will become Sheikh of Dhalkur.' That wouldn't be far off, given how poorly her uncle seemed.

The man before her inclined his head. 'That's certainly what Prince Fuad wants.'

His gaze dropped, surveying her from head to bare feet. Tara had to work not to twitch her toes in embarrassment. She wished she were wearing something classy and sophisticated. Something more than a cotton wraparound dress.

Sheikh Raif ibn Ansar didn't look at her the way Fuad did. There was nothing obviously sexual in that stare. Yet suddenly she was aware that they were alone together. That he was the most overtly masculine man she'd ever met. And that he made her aware of her femininity even now, when disaster crowded in on her.

'Your blood tie to the crown is stronger than his.' His voice, deep and musing, sounded far too appealing.

Tara's fingernails bit into the silk upholstery of her chair. There *had* apparently been muttered protests about Fuad inheriting the throne. The complaints were about his character and ability to lead the nation but not, as far as she knew, about the fact that his father, the current Sheikh, had been adopted by Tara's grandfather.

'People say that *yours* is the truly royal bloodline,' her interrogator murmured.

'No! My uncle was legally adopted and became my grandfather's heir. The royal council accepted it.'

Her mother had privately revealed that Tara's grandfather, the old Sheikh, had been so heartbroken when his first wife died that he'd refused to remarry to father a male heir, even though his daughter couldn't inherit the throne. In the end, bowing to pressure, he'd married his best friend's widow, adopting her son as his. The marriage and adoption were legal. But, according to her mother, the marriage was never consummated because the Sheikh couldn't bring himself to sleep with a woman other than his first wife.

Tara had thought the secret story terribly romantic. Like her parents falling in love at first meeting.

The fact remained that Tara's grandfather had gone to enormous lengths to secure the royal succession. She had no intention of becoming a pawn for those who tried to complicate it now. Especially as she had no desire to remain in Dhalkur.

'My home and my life are in Britain,' she said crisply. 'The current, legitimate Sheikh has two sons. Either could inherit the throne.'

Yet it was Fuad, the eldest, who was most likely to ascend the throne. Especially as his brother Salim was away overseas. Knowing Fuad, he'd try to keep Salim away till after the coronation.

Then there was his plan to use Tara, and especially the inheritance she hadn't known about till a week ago, to boost his position. Her stomach churned whenever she thought about it, a reaction that had nothing to do with her long, uncomfortable journey.

'So, *Ms Michaels*.' Tara felt her tension unravel a little now that the Sheikh had dropped the title that was so foreign to her. 'If you lost your passport, why not report it and get a new one?'

She met that obsidian-dark stare and knew she should have an answer ready. Yet the stresses of the day had sapped her inventive powers. She'd never had reason to lie in the past and it didn't come easily now.

'I...'

'Yes?' Elbows on the arms of his chair, he steepled his hands beneath his chin, as if waiting to consider her answer.

Did he have any idea how daunting he was? With his piercing gaze and the low, coaxing voice that encouraged the sharing of secrets yet barely concealed what she guessed was razor-sharp intelligence.

This man would see through any fumbling lie she proffered.

'Are you a friend of my cousin?'

'Why?' His expression didn't alter yet Tara *felt* the difference in him. As if suddenly he was on high alert.

'I'm curious.' Tara kept her gaze steady and her chin up, as if a quiver of nerves wasn't racketing through her taut body.

'You think that's sufficient reason to pry into personal matters?'

Tara was about to retort that he was prying into her life, but the situation wasn't the same. She was the one who'd sneaked into his country, his very palace, breaking who knew how many laws.

When she didn't reply he lifted his shoulders. 'I know your uncle and both your cousins. I wouldn't say I'm a friend of Fuad.'

Her shoulders dropped a fraction. If he wasn't a friend then perhaps there was a chance.

'And Salim?'

His honed features seemed to tighten, as if he was annoyed by her effrontery in questioning him. But what could she lose? She already faced the worst if he deported her back to Dhalkur.

After what seemed an eternity he spoke. 'Again, I don't know Salim intimately. I wouldn't call myself a friend. But I respect him.'

There'd been no mention of him respecting Fuad. Because he wasn't a fan, or because he was playing some double bluff, trying to entice her into revealing too much? These last couple of days she hadn't known who she could trust, until the unexpected meeting with Yunis and his offer of help.

Tara's head, still thick from the effects of her journey, began to throb.

'You were about to tell me why you didn't simply apply for a new passport.'

He was determined to get an answer, wasn't he?

'I didn't actually *lose* my passport.' She snatched in a quick breath then kept talking before her courage failed. 'Fuad confiscated it and refused to give it back.'

Saying the words brought it all back, the disbelief and horror. Her voice wobbled on the words and she looked down at her hands, pleating the material of her skirt. She smoothed out the fabric then placed her hands on the arms of her chair, trying to appear calm even though she wasn't.

'Are you going to explain?' Impatience threaded his voice.

'It depends. Are you going to send me back?'

'Clearly you don't want to return. But before I decide what to do with you, I demand an explanation. Especially,' his dark eyes pinioned her, 'if I'm to expect fallout from Dhalkur. I don't want an international incident. Your uncle and I have worked hard to improve relations between our countries, but old grievances still simmer and it will be some time before I'd call our relationship friendly.'

He sounded so reasonable. As if she were being paranoid. But the last week had turned her view of the world as basically safe and normal totally on its head. And she knew nothing of this man.

'Truly, I never meant for any sort of incident. I was hoping to get clear away without being discovered.'

'Without a passport or money?'

His gaze raked her light cotton dress and simple sandals, as if noting her lack of even a handbag.

Tara did have money with her, tucked into her bra

with her driver's licence, but she wasn't going to reveal that.

She shrugged. 'I didn't have much choice. I was a prisoner and I had the chance to get away, so I took it.'

When he said nothing, just watched her with that glittering gaze, she knew she had no option but to tell him everything, or at least enough to satisfy him.

She spread her hands. 'My mother died last month and about ten days ago I had a visit from representatives of the Dhalkuri embassy in London. They had a message from my uncle, asking me to return to sort out some of my mother's affairs. A few days later, after I'd arranged some time off work, I travelled with them to Dhalkur. I saw my uncle and Fuad and talked to a lawyer about a…bequest from my mother.'

No need to go into detail about the property her mother had inherited from Tara's grandfather and never mentioned, or that her solicitor in London didn't know about. The property which was now worth a fortune because of the rare earth metals discovered there, ready to be mined.

'I was a guest at the palace and at first I felt welcome.' For about a day, until Fuad's bizarre announcement. 'My uncle is very ill and Fuad has taken charge.'

The palace had an entirely different feel to the last time she'd visited. The servants didn't smile and the large kennel of pure-bred hunting dogs, her uncle's pride and joy, was empty. Fuad had ordered the dogs be got rid of—destroyed if homes couldn't be found for them. He'd always hated them, because they, and most animals for that matter, didn't like him.

'Go on.'

Tara looked up, dragging herself back from old memories.

'On the second day Fuad announced that he intended to marry. He said it would bolster his reputation as a solid leader to have a wife and potentially a family on the way. He said the country didn't want a repeat of the insecurity when my grandfather didn't have a clear male heir for so long.'

'He believes marrying will advance his cause beyond his brother's?'

Tara was on the point of saying *nothing* would make Fuad a better prospect than his brother, then recalled she didn't yet know how far she could trust this man.

'He seems to think so. He also thought, for the reasons you've mentioned, that marrying into my grandfather's bloodline would cement that advantage.'

She swallowed hard, trying to remove the bitter tang from her tongue.

'In other words, he wants to marry *you*.'

Did that unreadable face change? Did she imagine the tiniest flare of something in those midnight eyes?

It would be nice to believe him sympathetic but she couldn't count on it.

'Yes. He does.'

She shivered at the memory of Fuad's expression when she'd turned him down. And later, how anger had melded with a possessive hunger that frightened her to the core.

'I couldn't go to my uncle for help. He's too sick.' Tara looked down at her hands. 'He's dying.'

She'd never been close to him but he'd been kind over the years in his own way. His views on women

were old-fashioned, but he'd be horrified to know of
Fuad's threats.

'I know. I'm sorry.'

There it was again. Something in the Sheikh's tone
drew her eyes up to meet his and she had the impression that stern face fleetingly softened.

Was it an illusion because she desperately needed
this man's sympathy?

He looked like someone who'd never be bullied by
her cousin. He looked like the sort of man who...

No, she had no time for feminine fantasies. Her situation was too desperate.

Tara hurried on. 'Fuad threatened to keep me prisoner till I agreed to marry him.'

That wasn't all he'd threatened. He'd made pointed
reference to her small size and strength compared with
his. He'd been determined to claim her, one way or
another.

Another shiver skated down her spine and her nostrils flared as she remembered the smell of him when
he'd grabbed her arms in a vice-like grip and thrust his
face towards hers. Only the appearance of a messenger from his father's doctor had made him break away.

That was when Tara realised she had to make a run
for it. Fuad wasn't making empty threats.

She already knew about men who grabbed what
they wanted from helpless women.

'Ms Michaels? Tara?'

She looked up to find the Sheikh leaning forward,
his brow pleated. In concern?

Their gazes locked and Tara had the strangest feeling of connection. Of understanding.

Then, abruptly, he sat back and the moment shattered.

'He can't touch you here. You have my word on it.'

'Thank you.' Blood rushed through her body, her ears filled with the sound. She swallowed, her throat suddenly scratchy. 'Does that mean you won't send me back?'

Raif looked into clear green eyes that looked huge in that tense face and felt an unwilling pang of sympathy.

Initially it had been her pouting mouth that had drawn him. And, yes, that small but utterly feminine body. Now, so close he saw every emotion flitting across her features, he discovered Tara Michaels' expressive eyes were her most potent weapon.

Ever since she'd appeared at his feet, like a surprise birthday gift unwrapped for his pleasure, he'd had difficulty focusing on anything else. Even while he was questioning Yunis, the head of the master weavers' cooperative who'd delivered her to the palace, part of Raif's mind had been back in this room with this runaway.

'No. You're safe for now.'

'For now?' She leaned towards him, hands clasped together as if in prayer. 'What do you mean? What are you planning to do?'

Raif raised one hand. 'Be calm. I've promised you'll be safe in my home. You must be content with that while I decide what's to be done.'

Already she was shaking her head, her dark hair, which she'd secured in a long plait, sliding over one shoulder. Raif refused to watch the way it teased her breast. 'I know what's best. I need to return home immediately, to England.'

'Why? Is someone waiting there for you? A man who can protect you?'

Where had that come from? Yet he found himself canting forward, waiting for her answer.

'I don't need a man to protect me.' She sat straighter, as if to make up for her diminutive size. 'I can look after myself.'

Raif refused to say the obvious, that she hadn't been able to do so up till now.

But that was unfair. She'd been isolated in the royal palace. The royal servants would have done Fuad's bidding even if they didn't approve of his actions. With his father terminally ill and failing more each day, his was the power behind the throne. Raif's contacts across the border had already reported a number of troubling changes as Fuad sought to establish authority in the country.

Not for the first time Raif wished Fuad's younger brother, Salim, were home. Raif didn't interfere in politics across the border but it was obvious Dhalkur would be unstable under Fuad's temperamental influence. As for the years of work Raif had put into improving relations between the countries…

He suppressed a sigh.

He'd need to tread carefully. This was a complication he didn't relish.

Yet he knew he'd never hand Tara Michaels to her cousin.

It made sense not to give the man a bride who might win him the sheikhdom. But Raif knew it wasn't the future of the sheikhdom influencing him.

It was her expression, alternating between determination and vulnerability. That proudly firm chin, betrayed by the tiniest wobble of dismay. Those pouting lips, downturned now in disapproval. That body, petite but perfectly formed.

Silently Raif cursed. For he felt his body's quickening. The desire not just to protect the victim of a bully, but also to taste this woman's passion.

Would that mouth be as soft as it looked? Would those rapidly rising breasts fit his hands as exactly as he imagined?

His jaw tightened, muscles flexing hard as he banished the unruly thoughts. Raif never let lust override logic. Attraction and passion could be enjoyed, but always within set limits.

Besides, she needed help. Not another man slavering over her. He had no doubt Fuad's interest in his cousin wasn't solely for political reasons. The woman was a pocket Venus.

Disgusted at his thoughts, Raif concentrated on what must happen next. He had yet to confirm the details of her story. His contacts in Dhalkur had mentioned the arrival of the Sheikh's niece but she hadn't appeared in public. Raif needed to check that this was the same woman.

'Yes or no, Ms Michaels? Have you a protector in England?'

Fire simmered in her bewitching eyes. Her mouth turned mutinous. 'No.'

Raif exhaled slowly, telling himself it wasn't relief he felt that she didn't have a man in her life. It was no business of his, except in so far as she might have a champion.

'But the law will protect me there. I—'

'Tell me,' he broke across her protest, 'these representatives from the embassy who visited your home, they were men?'

'Yes.' She looked puzzled.

'Old or young?'

'Young.'

'Two young men. Fit-looking?'

'I… Yes, I suppose so.'

'And your flight from the UK was with a commercial airline?'

'No.' She was frowning now. 'It was on a private jet from a small airport.'

Raif nodded. 'Did it not occur to you to wonder why your cousin should send two people to invite you to Dhalkur? Surely one would do? Even a phone call from a lawyer.' He paused as he saw his words sink in. 'Instead he sent two young, presumably strong, men to your home.'

'You think if I hadn't agreed to go they'd have abducted me?'

Her face paled and Raif almost regretted stripping away her illusions. But her safety depended on it.

'I think Fuad leaves little to chance. He knows what he wants and he's determined to get it.'

'You don't think I'll be safe in London.'

'I don't.'

He watched her swallow, her hands clenching against the vivid crimson of her dress.

'I…see.' For a moment he caught a quiver on her lips before she flattened them and looked away, staring wide-eyed across the room as if she'd never before seen a potted orchid. Or was it the bookcase beyond that she stared at?

When she turned back her eyes looked glassy but she was calm, except for those restless hands knotting and unknotting in her lap.

'That complicates things. I'm afraid I'm not quite sure what to do now.'

Unwilling admiration stirred. He'd heard of the British stiff upper lip. Given her situation, her desperate escape attempt and her dramatic entrance, he wouldn't have been surprised if she'd succumbed to tears. He was profoundly grateful she hadn't. He abhorred shows of feminine emotion.

Which was still no reason to take a hand in this.

Raif didn't interfere with Dhalkuri politics. It was the first rule of good international relations.

Yet this woman was, however unintentionally, a guest under his roof. She deserved protection.

He *wanted* to protect her.

The thought of returning her to Fuad's less than tender mercies made his mouth curl at the sour taste on his tongue.

As did the idea of handing the man an asset, in the form of a bride, who'd help win the throne. Raif would far prefer it if Fuad's brother, Salim, inherited. A sensible, capable ruler rather than an unstable, egotistical one.

'For now, you don't have to worry about that. Rest here tonight and we'll meet tomorrow to discuss your options.'

CHAPTER THREE

TARA SOAKED HER stiff body in a deep bath. Even her arms finally stopped aching in the warm water. Dark bruises encircled her upper arms from when Fuad had tried to force himself on her.

That was in the past. Thanks to the Sheikh.

He seemed decent, if remote. There was no reason to believe him in league with her cousin. If so, surely he'd have packed her back to Dhalkur straight away.

Yet exposure to Fuad had made her wary. Politics was a devious game. She remembered her cousin's covetous look when he talked of her inheritance. Perhaps Sheikh Raif wanted a share of that? How much did he know about her?

Tara firmed her lips and sank back in the soothing water.

She had no option but to accept his offer of a bed for the night. She'd just have to be on her guard while she worked out her next step.

Except she had no idea what that would be.

Anxiety skated through her.

Technically London was home, so it had made sense to head there. Except Sheikh Raif had shown her how that might play into Fuad's grasping hands.

She gnawed her lip, pondering where she'd be safe.

London felt like a temporary stopgap. She and her mother had moved there after the mining accident in Africa that killed her father. Before that they'd lived in Asia, Australia and South America—wherever his work took him.

Maybe that was why Tara had felt restless in Britain. She was used to moving on. London was invigorating but the clouds and damp got her down. She longed for wide skies and warmth.

She'd been tempted to move from the UK in search of adventure but then her mother was diagnosed with cancer and Tara had shelved any thought of travel till her mother recovered. But after four years there'd been no recovery.

Her chest squeezed. Memories crowded, her beloved mum fading before her eyes. Yet she'd been indomitable to the end, making Tara promise to make the most of her life when she was gone.

Tara swallowed the familiar knot of hot grief that clogged her throat.

She loved her job as sales clerk for a top-class jeweller, but going back to her old routine didn't feel like making the most of life. Once she'd had plans to study and become a gem expert but that seemed a long time ago.

Tara sighed and let her head sink back. Scented steam curled around her, courtesy of the maid's lavish hand, scattering bath salts and rose petals.

The last few years she'd had little time to rest. At work she'd had to hide her emotions and be the consummate professional. At home and then at the hospice, she'd put on a brave face, talking about future travel plans, or outings with friends, anything to see her mother smile and relax.

After her recent stresses, Tara could handle some decadent luxury. Yet she felt like an imposter here. She was a sheikh's granddaughter but she'd never felt royal, never experienced such luxury, even at the Dhalkuri palace.

When Tara was shown to this suite with its court-yard, sitting room, dressing room and bathroom with a tub the size of a small swimming pool, she'd been ready to protest that there'd been a mistake. But tired-ness had won out.

She'd had an ultra-quick shower, then fallen into blessed oblivion, sleeping the afternoon away, till a maid brought tea and honey pastries.

Sheikh Raif's hospitality made her think more kindly of him. Even if he looked down that handsome nose at her. And made her uncomfortably self-aware.

Tara frowned. Strange how different his regard was to Fuad's. Her cousin had stared at her in a hungry way that made her feel like ants swarmed across her skin.

Once or twice she'd seen something in Sheikh Raif's eyes that made her body heat. He'd sized her up with the swift judgement of a connoisseur of women. Yet, despite that, and his ability to infuriate her, he hadn't made her feel that dreadful skin-crawling sensation she experienced with Fuad.

Or on that night when she was seventeen and her date spiked her drink. Someone had seen what hap-pened and rescued her before he could assault her. Yet she retained a horribly vivid memory of his leer as he reached for her while she'd been unable to move or de-fend herself. That awful sense of ceding control still haunted her dreams. It had been reignited this week under Fuad's threats.

Yet, here in Nahrat, Tara's body came to life in new and disturbing ways under the Sheikh's dark gaze.

It was remarkable. For years she'd been wary of men, especially attractive ones, like the guy who'd doped her. Yet caution wasn't her first instinct around the Sheikh.

She shifted, acutely aware of the warm water caressing her body, the tug and lap of it against bare skin.

Tara thought of hooded black eyes, proud features, so severe they shouldn't be handsome but were. The man was powerful, macho and used to getting his own way.

Her heart raced. What would it be like to be wanted by a man like that?

She couldn't believe she even wondered. Surely he was the sort to impose his will on a woman.

A husky chuckle escaped as she realised her foolishness. She'd never find out how it felt. He saw her as a political hot potato, not a potential lover.

Which was good. If ever she sought a lover it wouldn't be someone like Raif of Nahrat, so proud he'd probably click his fingers to summon his latest woman.

Yet that wasn't right. Something about his eyes and sensual mouth betrayed the ascetic's face. Tara imagined he'd be a demanding lover but a generous one.

Suddenly she was tingling all over. Beneath the warm water her nipples budded and between her legs there was a tiny ache.

Horrified, she surged to her feet and reached for a towel.

Her clothes had been removed for washing. In their

place was a long caftan of silk so fragile it felt like a butterfly's wing. It was of deep amethyst, embroidered in gold around the neckline with its deep central slit, and around the wide wrists. Instead of her sandals there was a pair of delicate slippers, covered in embroidered amethyst silk.

She'd never possessed anything so fine.

After a second's hesitation Tara lifted the dress over her head. The silk on bare flesh felt decadently luxurious, making her once more hyper-aware of her body.

Tara huffed her self-disgust. First she'd been unsettled by Sheikh Raif, and now by new clothes and a temporary lack of underwear. She was in a strange place with strange clothes and people she didn't know. That was all. Tomorrow morning, when she had her own belongings back, she'd feel herself again.

Flipping her hair back over her shoulders, she opened the door and crossed the bedroom. She needed a computer to check flights.

If only she knew where she was going. Once more fear curdled her insides. Fuad had power on his side and she didn't even have a plan.

'Hello, Tara.' The deep voice stopped her on the threshold of the sitting room.

She blinked, taking in the darkening night sky through the windows and the cosy glow of lamps.

A figure rose from where he sat on the far side of the room. He wore a suit. The top button of his shirt was undone, its crisp white fabric accentuating the dark gold of his flesh.

Tara's heart beat high and hard. She told herself it was a natural fight or flight response to finding a stranger in her rooms.

Except she'd known his identity instantly. That voice was unmistakeable. Even when he'd jabbed questions at her and looked disapproving, Sheikh Raif's voice had warmed her insides, making her think of dark, rich coffee and pastries dripping honey syrup.

Of addictive treats and secret cravings.

She pressed a hand against her swift-beating heart, then dropped it as the silk she wore pulled across her unfettered breasts, reminding her she was naked beneath the single layer.

That did nothing for her composure.

'I hope you don't mind if I call you Tara. It seems likely that you'll be here for some time.' He didn't move closer, but remained near the entrance to her suite.

As if waiting for her to invite him in?

It would be nice to think so. To forget that, as absolute ruler of this country, and owner of this vast palace, he could go where he chose.

Another tickle of doubt stirred. *Could* she trust him?

Gathering her scattered wits, Tara crossed the room, noticing things she'd missed in those first moments. Like the small dining table drawn up near a window, with place settings for two.

Like the way the mellow lighting accentuated the strong lines of his face and gleamed on his dark hair.

'Of course.' What choice did she have? At the moment he was her only protection against Fuad. She wouldn't antagonise him by refusing such a simple request, even if it felt safer when he called her Ms Michaels.

'And in private you may call me Raif.'

Tara blinked. She may not be a real princess but she

knew enough of her mother's family to understand this was an extraordinary privilege.

He must have read her face. 'You have a problem with that? It's not a difficult name to say.'

The corner of his mouth hooked up, as if her reluctance amused him. Could he read her so easily? Or did she imagine it? Now his expression was infuriatingly inscrutable, as it had been earlier.

'I'm just surprised.' She paused and swiped her tongue around her suddenly dry mouth. 'Thank you… Raif.'

Tara stepped closer.

'Has something happened? You said I might be here for some time.' She'd hoped to be on her way quickly, putting as much distance as she could between herself and Fuad. A single border wasn't enough.

Now she did read the Sheikh's… Raif's expression. The raised eyebrow, then a tiny nod, as if of approval.

'Please, sit and be comfortable while I explain.' He gestured to the dining table. 'I took the liberty of arranging to eat with you since we have more to discuss.'

Tara felt a flurry of nerves.

Because he had news she needed to sit down for? Or at the thought of dining with this man who made her more viscerally aware of herself as a woman than anyone she'd met?

'Of course.' She took the chair he indicated while he made a brief call on his phone.

'Dinner will arrive shortly.'

He settled opposite her and Tara had the uncomfortable realisation that, even up close and wearing the western clothes she was used to, he stood out from other men.

It wasn't just her imagination.

She opened her mouth to ask what had happened, when a knock on the door interrupted her.

The staff must have been waiting for his call. For the next few minutes cold drinks and an array of dips, breads, and other starters were placed before them. Then a man in a chef's uniform wheeled in a heat-proof trolley and revealed an array of succulent skewered meats and vegetables. The aroma of herbs and charcoal roasting made Tara salivate. It was a long time since her afternoon snack.

When the attendants left Raif said, 'I thought it best to serve ourselves in private. We won't be interrupted.'

His words evoked a memory of Fuad, who'd been eager for privacy with her. Wariness stirred.

Tara's gaze shifted from the food to the man. There was nothing lascivious in his regard. Raif—it worried her how easily she adapted to using his name—wasn't talking about seduction but business.

She smiled, her tight shoulders easing as she accepted a plate.

'I'm convinced the safest place for you to be for the foreseeable future is here, in my palace.'

'Define foreseeable future.' She looked at his stern features, remembered he was the supreme authority in this country and added, 'Please.'

'Until the next Sheikh is proclaimed.'

The serving spoons she was using clattered onto a plate of chargrilled vegetables.

'But that could take...' Tara shook her head. 'I thought maybe a day or two to sort myself out,' and, if he'd help her, to obtain a passport. 'I want to be well away from Dhalkur.'

'Fuad can't reach you here. You're safe under my protection.' Raif helped himself to salad and grilled lamb.

But Tara couldn't be so sanguine. 'I can't stay indefinitely.' Bad enough to feel beholden to this man for a short stay. To linger… The idea made her uncomfortable.

Straight black eyebrows lifted and his features took on an austere expression that made her wonder if he felt insulted.

'I'm so grateful for your help, Your M… Raif. It's wonderful to know my cousin can't reach me. But I need to go home.' Long enough to sort out her affairs, including her job, and find a bolthole outside the city.

'Because someone is waiting for you?'

Tara frowned. That was the second time he'd asked.

'No. No one.' Stupidly her throat constricted on the word and heat prickled her eyes, making her blink. She had friends in London but it was her mother who filled her mind.

'Forgive me.' His voice was surprisingly gentle. 'That was thoughtless. You mentioned your mother died last month. I didn't mean to dredge up painful thoughts.'

Meeting his steady gaze, she saw genuine regret.

It was unexpected. It made him suddenly more real. Not merely an autocratic leader or an astonishingly sexy man, but someone as human as she. Someone who made missteps and regretted them.

'It's fine. I like thinking of her.' Yet her smile wobbled. Because now there were so few people she could talk to about her mum. 'She was a special woman.'

'I'm sure she was, to produce such an indomitable daughter.'

Tara's eyes widened. Her? Indomitable? She'd been scared of Fuad and nervous about the trip here; all she could think of was how weak and vulnerable that made her.

'You don't think so?' Raif gestured with the serving spoons, and when she nodded began filling her plate.

She shrugged. 'I'm pretty ordinary.'

His smile took her by surprise. It began at the corner of his mouth, a tiny crook of amusement that slowly extended, curving his lips and creasing his lean cheeks into an expression that made her heart patter too fast. Even his eyes seemed to glitter more brightly as he surveyed her.

'Believe me, that entrance of yours was anything but ordinary. My poor chamberlain still hasn't recovered from the shock.' He put down the servers and sat back, his gaze catching hers, making a little pool of heat simmer deep inside. 'You didn't let that daunt you. You were as proud as any princess I've met.'

For a second longer Tara let the unfamiliar but invigorating heat spread and dance in her veins. Then she shook her head.

'I told you, I'm no princess.' After hearing her mother speak of the restrictions of royal life she was glad to be a commoner. 'I need to get back to London to ask my employer for more leave. To pack my flat up and rent it out while I find somewhere Fuad can't reach me.' Easier to say that than admit Raif's kingdom felt too close to her cousin.

'Ah.' Raif took a sip of sparkling water then put his glass down.

'What is it?' Tara had a bad feeling. 'You've had some news, haven't you?'

Those straight shoulders shrugged. 'My people have done some checking, which was made easier with your driving licence. Thank you for that.'

Tara nodded. She'd realised it would be easier for Raif to check her story with proof of identity.

'So you know for sure I am who I say I am.'

'Indeed. Sources in Dhalkur confirm something significant happened at the palace. Staff are on alert. Guards are patrolling the streets, searching premises and vehicles. There's a heightened presence at transport hubs and border crossings.'

No trace of a smile on Raif's face now. That lovely warmth she'd felt at being labelled indomitable faded. She found herself rubbing her hands along her silk-clad arms as a chill enveloped her.

'He's looking for me.' Her voice emerged husky.

'He is. But he won't find you. If you stay here.'

Tara heard the certainty in Raif's voice, felt its reassurance. Yet it wasn't enough.

'I need to get well away from Fuad. It's wonderful of you to help me but I can't impose—'

'Because you want to go back to your normal life.'

She nodded. Even if she had to go somewhere else, where Fuad couldn't locate her.

'I'm afraid that's not possible. Not yet.'

'Why not?'

'My staff report that your flat is under surveillance by men from the Dhalkuri embassy.'

Tara's stomach dropped, the morsel of food she'd eaten turning to lead.

'Fuad is already looking for me in London?' Of course he was. Why hadn't she thought of it sooner?

'More than that.' Raif's expression was grim. 'The Dhalkuri government has put out an alert for you. It's requested information if you cross the border into Nahrat and we understand they made the same request of the British authorities. Presumably they didn't stop there. Who knows which other countries have been contacted?'

Tara's fingers clawed at the fine linen tablecloth.

'I haven't done anything wrong! I'm not a criminal.'

'You left the country without a valid passport. But they haven't gone through Interpol, presumably because Fuad doesn't want to trump up fake criminal charges if he plans to marry you.' She fought a shudder at the thought. 'There's no warrant for your arrest. But, given you're part of the royal family, any such request would be considered seriously by other countries.'

Tara shook her head. 'I'm not royal. Fuad never thought so in the past.' Years ago, he'd taken delight in telling her how unimportant she was, her only link to the old Sheikh being through the female line.

Raif didn't bother to argue that point. 'While the UK government is unlikely to hand you over without a hearing, we both know Fuad will bypass the law if he can. Once he knows where you are…'

Raif let the sentence dangle but she had no trouble finishing it.

Once Fuad knew where she was he'd force her to return. He was devious and determined. Inevitably her mind conjured images of being bundled, gagged and bound, into a car and taken to a private airfield and a private plane. Of being helpless, unable to protect herself.

Pain seared her chest as her lungs tightened.

'Tara.' She blinked as warmth blanketed her clenched fists. She looked down to see Raif's hand, large, tanned and capable, covering hers.

She looked up and his dark eyes captured hers. 'Don't panic.'

She swallowed. 'It's hard not to. This is like something out of a thriller movie.'

'Except this will end quietly and calmly. Your uncle only has a week or so left.' Tara opened her mouth to ask how he knew, then shut it. Raif would be well-informed of major events in the region. He'd already mentioned information gained from sources in Dhalkur. Sources that didn't want Fuad to inherit?

'You need to wait till the new Sheikh is crowned. Once he's in control Fuad won't need to marry you to establish himself.'

Except it wasn't just her royal links her cousin coveted. He also wanted access to the wealth she'd inherited.

But maybe Raif was right. Maybe once Fuad became Sheikh he'd be too busy running the country to worry about her.

'When that happens, I'll arrange a new passport for you and put you on a plane to London.' His mouth curved in a reassuring smile. 'Meanwhile, for the next couple of weeks, you'll stay here incognito as my personal guest.'

CHAPTER FOUR

SLOWLY, ALMOST RELUCTANTLY, Raif released her hand and sat back.

That reluctance was unexpected and he didn't like it.

Ignoring the tingling on his palm, he reached for her glass and held it out to her.

'Drink,' he ordered. 'You'll feel better.'

He had no idea if she would, but he didn't like seeing her distressed.

A warning sounded in his brain.

This woman was a complication he didn't need.

True, he'd do anything to prevent Fuad inheriting. But interfering in Dhalkuri politics came at a cost. That was why there was animosity between the countries. For centuries both nations had tried to take control of the other, either overtly or behind the scenes.

Two generations ago there'd almost been war between them. Raif's grandfather had broken with centuries of royal tradition and married for love. Totally besotted with his bride, who hankered after life in the international jet set instead of a dutiful one, he'd ignored everything but her. The country had been left wide open for Dhalkuri infiltrators and insurgents. War had only just been averted and the damage to the country had taken years to overcome. It was only when Raif's father took the throne that the nation really recovered.

Relations were, at best, wary, though Raif and the Sheikh of Dhalkur had worked to increase cooperation.

Tara Michaels, with her big eyes and obstinate chin, was trouble. Looking at her put him on alert.

In the seventeen years since he'd ascended the throne at thirteen, Raif had learned to think before he acted. His grandfather's errors had been held up by his mentors as a lesson in the dangers of following his heart instead of his head. But he was still a man who knew an opportunity when he saw it. A man who capitalised on such opportunities.

Besides, sheltering Tara Michaels wasn't simply about thwarting her cousin's plans. It was an act of simple decency. Raif had never warmed to the Sheikh of Dhalkur's eldest son. If the rumours about his temper and violent ways were even half true, Raif wouldn't leave a dog in his care, much less a woman.

Raif's determination to get involved had nothing to do with the clenching awareness he felt whenever he met Tara's clear gaze. Or the fact that each shuddering breath made her pert breasts rise hard beneath her gown.

That conservative garment should be an effective cover-up, but not when she forgot to wear a bra. He could see the points of her nipples and the way her breasts occasionally jiggled against the rich fabric, as if unrestrained.

Despite his good intentions she kept reminding him she was a desirable woman, not merely a diplomatic problem.

Was that why he'd reached across and held her hand?

The result had been a raking shudder of awareness.

Yet even that wasn't all of it. The lost look in those great eyes, her mix of fear and determination, had touched him in a way that was quite separate to her feminine allure.

'It's very kind of you to invite me to stay.' She bit the corner of her lip and Raif wished she wouldn't. It made him want to smooth that lush mouth. Even, perhaps, test it with his own.

Abruptly he pushed his chair back. Being in her suite wasn't a good idea. He'd organised a meal here, thinking of her comfort and keeping her presence secret. Now he realised his mistake.

Raif got to his feet. 'Make yourself at home. If there's anything you need you have only to ask my staff.'

'You're leaving?' She looked stunned and who could blame her? He'd eaten nothing.

But, aware that his growing appetite wasn't for food, he needed to leave. It was unacceptable to think of Tara as anything other than someone needing his help. Raif didn't take advantage of people under his protection.

Even if he was almost sure some of her covert glances were appreciative. Nor had he missed the quick thrum of the pulse at her wrist when he'd held her hand.

Of course her pulse quickened! She's worried about Fuad coming after her.

'I'm not hungry.' *Not for any of the dishes on the table.* 'I simply wanted to update you and assure you that you'll be protected.'

She rose, hands clasped together.

'I can't tell you how much I appreciate your help.

It's kind of you to help me. Especially given my unorthodox entry.'

She meant the way she'd sneaked across the border. But Raif's thoughts went to the memory of her, all golden limbs, long hair and lush curves, sprawled at his feet like some offering.

He drew a deep breath, feeling the blood of his ancestors pound through him. They'd been protectors of their people but also men with no compunction in claiming any prize that caught their eye.

Tara Michaels, with her small but emphatically feminine figure, her bright eyes and seductive pout, was enough to catch any man's eye.

Raif inclined his head, telling himself her looks didn't influence his actions. 'I'm happy to assist. My only condition is that you stay within the palace and out of public spaces. The fewer who know you're here the better.'

Tara prowled through the Courtyard of a Thousand Mosaics. But standing under a colonnaded walkway, as big and as beautiful as the cloisters of any cathedral, she barely took in its beauty.

Three days ago she'd discovered this place and been blown away by it.

Millions of exquisitely hand-painted tiles in shades of blue, green and gold decorated the floor, walls and even the bottom of the shallow pools in the centre of the garden. That colour scheme, the glossy-leaved citrus trees and the tinkling sound of a multitude of fountains, created a cool and peaceful ambience.

She'd been charmed. She'd been enchanted too with

the Sheikha's Rose Garden, where arbours heavy with fragrant climbing roses invited you to relax.

Then there was the Sheikh's private library, stocked with thousands of books in several languages. The gymnasium. The lap pool.

So many facilities at her disposal. All tempting, all gorgeous, and none satisfying.

Tara was going stir crazy.

She hadn't even been allowed to wash her own clothes. After her first night in the palace she'd woken in that comfortable-as-a-cloud bed to discover the wardrobe full of clothes and shoes, all in her size. There were western-style dresses, one of them like the crimson wraparound dress she'd worn when she arrived. Except the new one was in a vibrant green, of some clingy, fragile fabric. Then there were the long traditional dresses in jewel colours, each more beautiful than the last.

Yet, despite the luxury, without some occupation she felt like a prisoner.

Tara slumped onto a shaded seat. She had nothing to complain about and every reason to be thankful. She *was* thankful.

Her pulse galloped as she remembered being isolated in her uncle's palace, Fuad threatening retribution if she didn't give in to him.

But after four days cooped up, Tara longed for people to talk to, a purpose, even a change of scene.

She was too stressed to lose herself in a book. The staff were polite but kept their distance and the only other person she saw, briefly, was Raif. Every day he'd share coffee with her and update her on the latest news from Dhalkur. He'd ask if she needed anything and she'd say no. Then he'd nod and leave.

When he did, Tara felt even more alone.

Four days of luxurious isolation, following a week's imprisonment in Dhalkur, still felt like confinement.

Tara was used to being active. Working. Caring for her mother. Having responsibilities. But after a couple of phone calls, including to her work in London, asking for more leave, here she was, without a purpose.

She shot to her feet, annoyed at her moping. There must be some other place she could explore. Anything to pass the time that lay so heavy.

Tara was heading back through the private section of the palace when she noticed a door she hadn't seen before. Opening it, she discovered the sitting room where Raif had questioned her that first day. She must have been too upset then to take in the view from the long window.

A minute later Tara was out on the balcony, breathing deep and grinning from ear to ear. Her rooms were in the secluded centre of the palace. This wasn't secluded. This felt like freedom!

Before her was a wide strip of parkland and then the multi-coloured buildings of the old city. She was close enough to make out people on the streets below the ramparts of the citadel. Further away, new buildings and a forest of cranes attested to the capital's thriving commercial hub.

She heard traffic, a dog barking, watched a woman hanging out washing on a flat roof that doubled as a garden with pots of what might be herbs. Tara inhaled, catching the scents of the city and something delicious, as if the breeze blew from the old spice markets that she'd read were only a few streets away.

A boy and a dog galloped up the street that separated the palace from the city. A few minutes later another boy appeared with a football. Soon they were kicking the ball about in the open ground. In no time two impromptu teams had formed.

Tara leaned on the railing, her spirits lifting as she watched the game and the bustle of people. To be an unseen observer of the life in the city...

She blinked, her smile freezing, as one of the footballers pointed and several heads turned her way.

Instantly she stepped back from the railing.

What had she been thinking? She'd felt like an unseen observer but she wasn't invisible.

To her horror the balcony door didn't open easily from the outside. Was it stiff or had it automatically locked?

Eventually the latch turned with a click and she hurried inside, her heart racing as if she'd been part of that energetic football game. Her palms were damp as she shut the door. But one final look revealed that no damage had been done. The kids were engrossed in their game again and no one seemed to be looking this way.

It wasn't till the next morning that she discovered her mistake.

'His Majesty requests your presence in the audience chamber.' The chamberlain didn't quite meet her eyes and Tara remembered his shock when she'd tumbled out of the carpet in that very room.

'In the audience chamber?' Tara's nape prickled. Usually she met Raif in a sitting room or his office.

He hadn't returned to her suite since that first night and Tara tried not to mind his withdrawal. The man ruled a nation. She was an unwanted guest. Of course he had no time for her.

Even if she spent far too many hours thinking about him.

The chamberlain frowned and finally met her stare. He didn't look happy.

'Yes, he has a visitor, the Dhalkuri ambassador.'

Tara took an involuntary step backwards, bumping into the sofa from which she'd risen. Her hand went to her breastbone, to where her heart hammered.

'He's come to take me back!' Her voice stretched thin, her mind racing to avenues of escape. She'd even turned instinctively towards the doors leading onto the private courtyard, but there was no escape that way.

Fear flooded her, and frustration. She didn't even know where the exits were in this vast place.

'You have nothing to fear.' The words made her turn back. The few times she'd met the chamberlain he'd looked serious, if not disapproving. Now his expression softened. 'His Majesty will look after you.'

Even so, Tara trembled from head to foot.

She'd put her trust in Raif and now it would be tested. What did she really know of his motives?

'Very well.' She smoothed her hands down her thighs, realising she wore the same wraparound dress as when she'd arrived. Was that an omen that she was about to return? She told herself not to be fanciful. 'Give me a minute to tidy my hair.'

When the doors to the audience chamber were opened and the chamberlain led her in, Tara was glad she'd taken the time to put her hair up into a chignon.

She wished she'd also changed her clothes into something more sophisticated.

She felt daunted, not just by the opulence of the vast room decorated in white, royal blue and gold, but also by the men waiting for her. The ambassador stood grim-faced before the royal dais where Raif sat enthroned.

Tara tried to take heart from the fact he hadn't been invited to sit, that this was clearly a very formal interview, but instead that merely highlighted the seriousness of the moment.

She looked up at Raif, hoping for reassurance, but found his attention on the ambassador, not her.

Gone was any trace of the man who'd shared coffee and been kind, if in a slightly formal way. In his place was a monarch, imposing on his gilded throne. As she crossed acres of inlaid marble his face was unreadable.

Was the chamberlain right? Would Raif protect her? She was a stranger. Why should he risk harming his relationship with his closest neighbour for her sake?

'Ms Michaels.' Even his voice sounded different, portentous somehow.

'Your Majesty.' She curtseyed, only lifting her head when he spoke again.

'The Ambassador of Dhalkur has approached me with a representation from your cousin Fuad.'

'With respect, sir,' the ambassador said smoothly, 'from His Majesty the Sheikh.'

'Ah, from the Sheikh himself? Obviously I misunderstood. I believed the Sheikh's illness is so advanced he's no longer issuing instructions or messages and that his son is acting as his proxy. I'm glad to hear his illness is not so grave.'

The ambassador opened his mouth then closed it, looking discomfited. 'This is a private matter, sir. If I might speak alone with Ms Michaels.'

Tara clasped her hands together so she didn't wring them. She darted a glance in Raif's direction, wishing she could borrow some of his composure. Still, he didn't meet her gaze. 'I'd prefer to hear the message here,' she said.

The ambassador's head reared back. He hadn't expected that. Tough. Even here in Raif's palace she had no desire to be alone with Fuad's messenger.

The man cleared his throat. 'Your family asks that you return to the palace. Your uncle needs you and your cousin also charged me with saying he's concerned about you, alone, so far from home.'

'You may tell my cousin there's no need for concern. I'm comfortable and safe.' She paused, giving emphasis to the last word. 'As for my uncle needing me, I'm afraid there's some confusion. My uncle—'

'No confusion, I assure you.' Yet the ambassador wasn't looking at her but at Raif. 'Within these walls I can reveal that our beloved Sheikh is, in fact, very ill. Is it any wonder he wants Ms Michaels by his side?'

'Frankly, yes,' Tara answered, wiping the half-smile from the man's face. She turned to Raif, for some reason needing him to understand. 'My cousin rejected all my attempts to spend time with my uncle, even going so far as to give orders that I wasn't to be admitted to see him.'

That had hurt. She and her uncle weren't close, but the man was dying and she'd wanted to provide what support she could. What had Fuad feared might happen if she spent time alone with him?

'One day I did manage to see my uncle.' Because a kind nurse had let her slip in. 'But after a while he said that he preferred the ministrations of medical professionals. He made me promise not to come back to him.'

Her throat closed. What he'd actually said was that he didn't want his niece hanging around his deathbed. He'd been trying to protect her, as if she hadn't seen her own mother fade away before her eyes. He'd said his goodbyes and told her to leave.

Tara blinked and stood straighter. Her uncle was a decent man and the nearest she had to family now. She'd be sorry when he died.

The ambassador's eyes rounded but he pressed on. 'It's a very difficult time, to be sure. But all the more reason to draw close to your family, to offer your support as your cousins face this looming tragedy.'

For her cousin Salim it would be a tragedy. But for Fuad, his father's death would give him supreme authority, something he craved.

Tara's chin lifted. 'As they supported me when my mother died?' Her voice thickened. 'My cousin Fuad sent his condolences three weeks after her death. Even then, the message was primarily to summon me to discuss my mother's estate.'

Salim had contacted her straight away, offering support and sympathy. The difference between his concern and his brother's lack of it had been starkly obvious.

The ambassador's face grew mottled.

'There is also the question of your affairs. Such a significant inheritance would fit more naturally under the control of your male relatives. Used properly it will benefit the whole country.' He spread his hands and faced the throne. 'Far be it from me to accuse Ms

Michaels of lack of womanly sympathy or appropriate respect—'

'Good,' Raif said, his voice cutting. 'Because your role as ambassador doesn't give you the right to criticise Ms Michaels. Or pass judgement on what she should do with the land she's inherited. Or to make assumptions about recent circumstances which, I *hope*,' he leaned forward, 'you were not involved in.'

There was no mistaking the steel behind his smooth tone. Or the horror on the ambassador's face. Raif, his expression stern and gaze piercing, looked every inch the absolute ruler. A man used to wielding ultimate power.

Tara felt her breath shudder out in a sigh of relief. Raif had said nothing all this time and she'd begun to fear he'd side with the ambassador.

'But Your Majesty—'

'Do you have any further information to put before me, or perhaps something new to tell Ms Michaels?'

The ambassador goggled up at him. 'I was instructed to accompany her back personally.'

Raif nodded. 'A sensible arrangement. It's been brought home to me recently that women alone can be prey to all sorts of dangers.'

Tara stared up at him. Sensible? Surely he didn't mean to force her to go with this man?

'Your Majesty—' she began.

'If Ms Michaels chooses to return you'll be informed and can escort her personally. But as, at the moment, she plans to remain in Nahrat,' he turned to her and she nodded her confirmation, 'there's nothing more to be done than to thank you for your message and send our very best wishes to your Sheikh and his sons. I'm thinking of them at this difficult time.' He paused, then added, 'My chamberlain will see you out.'

The ambassador looked ready to protest, but Raif's implacable expression stopped him. The chamberlain ushered him out.

It wasn't till the pair had left that Tara filled her lungs with a deep, sustaining breath. Her hands, locked before her, were clammy and her heartbeat was loud in the silence.

She blinked and bowed her head, telling herself it was over. She was safe. Raif hadn't given her up, though his silence as the ambassador spoke had worried her.

Her legs wobbled terribly and she wished she had something to hang on to. But the only piece of furniture in the room was the gilded throne.

On the thought she looked up and movement caught her eye. Raif, rising from that imposing seat and stepping off the royal dais. He paced towards her and Tara shuffled her feet wider, stiffening her legs.

He didn't stop till he stood immediately before her and she arched her neck so she could meet his eyes. The man didn't need a dais. He was tall enough and imposing enough to impress without it.

'That was totally avoidable,' he said, in a low voice that lashed like a whip. 'Exactly what part of staying in the palace, out of the public eye, don't you understand?'

Raif looked into those clear green eyes, registered her flash of surprise, and felt anger ramp up.

Anger that he knew would be better directed at the bumptious ambassador or, better still, Prince Fuad, pulling strings to secure his runaway cousin. Yet his ire rose like a living, breathing beast within him.

It should never have come to this. Hadn't he *warned* her?

The sight of Tara, alone and seemingly fragile, facing down their visitor, had clutched at something deep inside Raif. At one point her mouth had crumpled, before she'd thrust her shoulders back and confronted her cousin's emissary. As he saw that sign of weakness Raif's belly had clenched and he'd had to force himself not to intervene and put himself between her and the ambassador.

That would have inflamed an already disastrous scenario.

This situation was fraught enough without him appearing as anything but impartial, in public at least. He might be supreme ruler of his own country but he trod a very delicate path, harbouring a foreign runaway. A *royal* foreign runaway.

Didn't she understand that?

The fact that he'd been forced to sit passively and allow that scene to play out had tested his endurance to the limit. Raif had wanted to take charge, deal with the ambassador and let diplomacy be damned.

His instinct to protect this woman was so compelling it went beyond a desire for justice and fair play. This was something different, more potent, and he didn't like it one bit. It felt like a form of weakness, and that fuelled his temper.

He was *not* weak. He'd never allow a woman to undermine his duty to his nation.

'I didn't go out. Truly. I've stayed in the palace the whole time.' Her chin jerked higher but now, instead of applauding her feistiness, Raif didn't like her attitude. She had no cause to look at *him* that way. He'd been the one to stop her being dragged back to Dhalkur.

He took a slow breath and fought the seething fury inside.

'No. Instead you flaunted yourself on the Sheikh's private balcony, the place where rulers appear to their people at major celebrations.'

Her mouth sagged open and Raif had the satisfaction of knowing she hadn't deliberately sabotaged the secrecy surrounding her stay. But that was no comfort, given the inevitable, severe repercussions.

He closed his eyes for a second, drawing on the reserves of strength that had seen him through years of diplomatic negotiations and ruling a country full of proud, opinionated, indomitable people.

It didn't help that when he looked down again Tara appeared put out, as if *he'd* done something wrong, not her.

'I didn't know it was your balcony. No one told me.'

He shook his head. What did she want? Signs at every door for her convenience, explaining the purpose of each space?

'The fact that it was clearly visible to the public should have stopped you. How do you think the Dhalkuri authorities discovered you were here? You were seen. Photos were taken. The press is humming this morning with the story of the strange woman in the palace.'

'I'm sorry. I didn't realise. I was restless after days being cooped up.'

If she'd looked repentant Raif would have ended it there. He dealt pragmatically with issues, not wasting time apportioning blame. But Tara Michaels stared back at him as if *he* were at fault. As if a few days as his pampered guest was some sort of trial.

What more did the woman want from him?

She'd already got under his skin to an alarming extent. He thought of her when he should be working, or sleeping. He found himself thinking about that sultry mouth of hers and how it would feel on his skin. Which in turn made him feel guilty.

He almost heard his patience snap.

'I gave you an instruction and you disobeyed me. Don't you *want* my help?'

She drew herself up straighter, as if from just below his shoulder she could stare him down. Her hands jammed onto her hips in an attitude designed to provoke.

'I'm not your servant.' Her tone was fire and ice, lashing at his skin and drawing it tight.

Raif felt his hands clench at his sides and his teeth grind. 'No, you're my guest. My uninvited guest.'

For a second he saw something unreadable flare in her eyes but before he could decipher it she spoke again, her lip curling disdainfully.

'If I'm such a burden, I'll leave. If you give me that passport you promised and show me the exit, I'll be on my way.'

Infuriating woman! As if she'd be going anywhere now. He'd had enough of her attitude.

She opened her mouth, no doubt to lambast him again, and it was too much.

In one swift movement he wrapped his arm around her waist and hauled her against him.

There! He almost heard his body's cry of relief. As

if he'd waited months to feel her against him instead of days. Her soft curves fitted perfectly in his embrace.

Her eyes were huge, her lips apart, but she didn't speak. Just looked up with something in her expression that sent a buzz of anticipation through him.

Raif waited a split second then surrendered to the force that had driven him since the moment she'd tumbled out of the carpet to lie so provocatively at his feet.

He bent his head and covered her mouth with his.

CHAPTER FIVE

IF SHE'D WANTED to stop him she could have. Raif's grip was firm but not unbreakable.

Instead Tara stood where she was. She might even have leaned towards him, her palms to his chest for balance. The feel of his hot, honed body beneath her hands sent a tremor of excitement through her. But that was nothing to the impact of his kiss.

There was no hesitation. No fumbling to get the right angle. Nor was it punishing, despite his anger.

Raif kissed like he seemed to do everything else: decisively. With impeccable talent.

Perfectly.

Tara swallowed a sigh of pleasure as his mouth possessed hers. It was persuasion and invitation and such pleasure. Inevitably she responded.

How could she not?

For days she'd been acutely aware of Raif, not just as a protector, but also as a man who drew her lonely body into tingling awareness. Even the warning voice of past experience, telling her that men weren't always as they seemed, died under his kiss.

This was better than any of her fervid imaginings.

Tara leaned closer, higher, hands fisting in his clothes and tugging him down to her.

The arm around her back tightened. Heat blossomed where she fitted between his thighs. Her wayward mind imagined them wedged together like this but without so many clothes, and suddenly she had trouble getting enough oxygen.

Raif's hand lifted to her jaw, her cheek. She felt the slight burr of calluses against her skin and shivered, her senses deliciously heightened. Long fingers pushed past her ear, into her hair, gripping, massaging, and delight whirled through her, making her shake and her knees loosen.

She inhaled the scent of male spice and sandalwood, absorbed the rich taste of him, and needed more.

Her hands rose up the back of his head to tunnel through thick hair, clamping his skull and holding tight.

A low sound vibrated from his mouth to hers, a deep, murmuring growl of masculine pleasure. Tara's nipples peaked hard against him, heat drilling down to that needy spot at the apex of her thighs.

Was this why she'd felt so ready to stand up to Raif? Almost taunting him when she could see he was annoyed? As if she *wanted* to spur his anger till he snapped. As if she hoped he felt this electric spark too.

That couldn't be it. Her anger had been justified. He had no right to order her about.

And yet…

And yet her righteous indignation died as he swept her close and made her feel things she couldn't remember ever feeling.

Desirable. Cherished. Powerful. As if she could

level mountains with a sweep of her hand. And lose herself utterly in this man's earthy desire.

This wasn't just a kiss. Their bodies strained together like twin halves of a long-separated whole, and it was blissful.

In fact, as she squirmed closer she felt…

Raif stepped back so abruptly she swayed, bereft of his anchoring frame.

He didn't reach out to support her. Instead he put even more distance between them, his brow scrunching into a mighty scowl. His hands clenched in fists at his sides.

Tara's heart skipped a beat then plunged. Hadn't he felt the magic?

Her ragged breathing was loud in her ears. Her heart hammered and a voice in her head told her to close the gap between them and kiss him again, because what they'd shared was too good to stop.

Where that voice came from she didn't know. In twenty-three years she'd never heard it before. Usually she heard a jangling alarm if she got close to intimacy. A warning to beware. Not this time.

Tara blinked up, transfixed by the change in Raif's expression. A shiver racked her and now it wasn't a hot shudder of excitement but cold, so cold.

He'd looked annoyed and impatient before. Then, in the seconds before he'd claimed her, she'd seen something flare in those dark eyes. Something reckless and eager.

Had she imagined it?

Now there was the downward tilt of his eyebrows and lips, deepening grooves bracketing a grim mouth and the flare of aristocratic nostrils as if they scented something unpleasant.

'That shouldn't have happened.' He stood stiffly. His jaw clenched as if with pain. Or disgust.

Disgust that he'd touched her?

A horrified shudder swamped Tara. She'd got it wrong.

Seconds ago she'd thought him aroused. Instead he'd kissed her out of pique. He'd been angry and didn't like her challenging him. So he'd silenced her.

And she'd let him. Worse, she'd loved every moment. Every touch, every breath, had been a revelation.

Because she had such limited sensual experience after years supporting her mother through the grief of losing her father, and then through illness?

'It *definitely* shouldn't have happened,' Raif repeated in case she hadn't got the message.

Because, of course, she wasn't the sort of woman the exalted Sheikh of Nahrat would kiss. She was an *uninvited guest*.

Had he really kissed her to stop her words? Or had he—the thought stirred a sick feeling in her stomach—simply been curious? After all, she wasn't like the sophisticates he usually mixed with.

Anger shot through Tara's blood and crawled across her skin, drawing it tingling tight.

'You're right.' She almost spat the words. 'It shouldn't. I don't want you touching me again. *Ever*. Is that clear?'

He might be a sheikh. He might have power, wealth and an unassailable aura of machismo. He might have an inflated view of his own worth, but he was *not* her superior. He was a man, as flawed as the next one. Nothing gave him the right to use her that way.

For all Tara knew he was no better than Fuad. The press reports she'd read about Raif were almost fawning, continually singing his praises. But none of them investigated the real man behind his royal authority.

'Don't worry! It's a mistake that won't be repeated.'

But Tara barely heard. Through the fog of anger and hurt, something the ambassador had said suddenly lodged in her brain. Something she should have noticed before.

'You knew,' she said in a strangled voice.

'Sorry?'

'You weren't surprised when the ambassador mentioned my inheritance. You didn't ask what he meant about the nation benefiting from it.'

Tara's eyes narrowed on the man before her. Was that discomfort on those strong features? It was impossible to tell.

'I don't see the problem. It's straightforward. Your mother died and left you property.' He folded his arms, emphasising his broad chest and his annoyance.

Tara stared back, crossing her own arms. 'It's more than that. You weren't surprised or interested because you already knew about it.' Her voice rose. 'You *knew* what my inheritance is. You mentioned land, not money or a house or something more general.'

Now Tara saw it. The shimmer of confirmation in his dark eyes, despite the fact his mouth remained as still and stern as before.

Dismay hit, hard as a fist to the ribs.

She'd escaped Fuad but now she was stuck in Sheikh

Raif's palace, unable to leave until he provided the passport he'd promised.

Awful doubt stirred in her belly then snaked through her, sending out slithery coils of fear.

Had she escaped one man determined to use her for his own ends, only to find herself at the mercy of another? A man who was simply better at hiding his motives? She should have guessed. Shouldn't have let herself be lulled into ignoring those hard-learned lessons about self-protection.

'So?' He looked utterly supercilious.

'How long have you known about my inheritance?'

'What does it matter? It's a minor point.'

Her stomach plunged towards the floor. He didn't want to answer. She had a terrible feeling she knew why. Because he, too, wanted to get his hands on her inheritance.

Why else hide her from her cousin? Why treat her as his personal guest and lavish such luxury on her?

The last couple of weeks she'd learned how far an unscrupulous man would go.

'Tell me,' she demanded. '*When* did you find out about the land I've inherited?'

Land which had recently been found to contain large quantities of rare and valuable substances. Usually found in very small deposits unsuitable for mining, this large deposit could be a huge boost to the economy, or, if Fuad married her, to his personal fortune, because under local law Tara owned both the land and its mining rights. If Fuad married her, he'd control both.

Finally Raif answered. 'I heard rumours of a significant find of rare elements weeks ago. I had confirmation around the time you arrived.'

Tara's chest cramped. She was right. A sour tang filled her mouth.

'You're well informed. Do you have spies in the Dhalkuri court?'

He shook his head. 'No spies. The find is no secret. I have business and diplomatic contacts through the region. It's no surprise I'd hear such significant news.'

Why hadn't Tara thought of that? Why had she assumed all he knew of her was what he'd discovered after she arrived?

'I should have known.' How foolish she'd been, trusting this man.

'Known what?'

She had to hand it to him. Raif did haughty like no one else. When Fuad aimed for hauteur he merely managed arrogant and thuggish. Tara looked up at the man before her and wondered what, if anything, would discomfort him.

Probably nothing. He had too high an opinion of himself.

'That this,' she waved her hand, 'your hospitality, comes at a price.' The thought of how he'd played her like a complete innocent spurred her indignation. It felt all the worse because she'd liked him.

More, she'd been attracted. His magnetic looks combined with his kindness had suckered her into believing he was on her side. Instead it seemed she was still stuck in the nightmare that had begun in Dhalkur.

Tara swallowed, pushing down a horrible feeling of self-pity, and concentrated on anger.

Raif's mouth thinned and his folded arms fell to his sides. 'What exactly are you saying, Tara?'

'It's an unlikely coincidence that you took me in,

a complete stranger, and went to such lengths to protect me. Especially when all the time you knew I have a potential fortune. A fortune I'm told would benefit any nation.'

She knew about grasping, predatory men. How had she allowed herself to forget?

For a second, for two, Raif merely stared down at her, eyes glittering and nostrils flaring.

Tara gave him a death stare of her own. She refused to let him intimidate her.

'Is that why you kissed me?' She had to stop and clear her thickening throat. 'Were you hoping I'd be so blown away that I'd fall under your spell? That you'd persuade me to give you access to my inheritance?'

Her mouth trembled so hard she bit her bottom lip to stop it quivering.

Because she *had* fallen under his spell. Even before the kiss she'd been fascinated by him. When he'd taken her in his arms she'd all but gone up in flames. Even now, racked with hurt and indignation, part of her yearned for his touch, his taste, the passion she'd discovered in his embrace.

How naïve she'd been.

Raif took a step towards her, his gaze like obsidian, black and hard.

'You really think,' he paused and shook his head, 'that I have designs on your inheritance?'

'Why not? My cousin does. Apparently this cache of minerals will bring the owner immense wealth.'

'And how, precisely, would my kindness give me access to that? Do you imagine I want to *marry* you for your money?' Disdain dripped from every syllable, puncturing Tara's certainty.

She hadn't thought that through. But surely there was something fishy here? To go from that kiss to such contempt?

'I don't know. I just know it's unlikely a man in your position would go to such lengths to help someone ordinary like me. But if you thought you could butter me up and do some deal to get access to the land…' She shrugged and spread her hands.

'This buttering up…it falls short of marriage, then. Is my dastardly plan to seduce you into sharing your mineral rights?'

When he put it like that, it sounded preposterous. But he was hiding something, she sensed it.

'You *did* kiss me.'

'Oh, well, in *that* case, I must be up to no good,' he sneered. 'It never occurred to you that you're a beautiful, infuriating woman and that even a man of honour might be goaded into unwise action as a result?'

Tara gaped at him. Beautiful and infuriating?

Raif thought her beautiful?

He shook his head. 'Of course you didn't. You're so fixated on your cousin you make the insult of assuming I'm like him. No!' he continued when she opened her mouth. 'Don't speak. You've already said more than enough. Come with me.'

He swung towards the door but Tara stood firm.

'Where are you going?'

'You think I want your wealth. Well, there's something you need to see.'

Tara had the uncomfortable feeling she had been at least a little ridiculous. And yet—

'Ow.' She flinched as he took her upper arm.

Raif scowled and released his hold. 'Do we need the dramatics? My grip wasn't tight.'

Tara blinked at the pain searing her arm.

'Tara?' Her face must have revealed her discomfort, for his expression altered. 'What is it?'

She shook her head but he was already lifting the soft cotton of her sleeve.

Tara knew what he'd see and for reasons she couldn't explain wished he wouldn't. Having anyone else view the massive bruises made her shrink inside.

Raif's face turned grim. His jaw had a hard line and a pulse throbbed at his temple.

Slowly, as if consciously not making a move that might startle her, he rolled up her other sleeve, while she stood motionless, wishing this was over.

'Fuad did this?'

Tara shivered. Not with cold, but because of a new note in Raif's soft voice.

She'd heard him annoyed. She'd heard him indignant and angry but that was nothing to the lethal note she heard now in that quiet tone.

She darted a look up but he was examining her arms. She turned her head. His fingers hovered above the ugly purple-blue bruises that were beginning to turn a lurid shade of green.

'Yes.' She shivered, swamped by the memory of Fuad grabbing her, shoving her up against the wall, threatening her. The way he'd pawed at her dress, only stopping when interrupted by someone with an urgent message, made her stomach turn.

'He'll pay for this.' Raif spoke so softly Tara almost didn't hear him, as he rolled her sleeves down to cover the discoloured flesh.

* * *

It was easier for Raif to concentrate on drawing Tara's sleeves back into place, than to meet her eyes.

Shame filled him, along with anger at the sight of her injuries. That shame was unfamiliar, a burning sour taste in his gullet.

He'd made his share of mistakes but couldn't recall anything to compare with this. Nothing to rival the potent whirl of guilt.

The sight of Tara's injuries sickened him.

But not as much as the realisation he'd lost control and hurt her. The throbbing pain and confusion in her voice as she'd accused him of using her gouged his conscience.

She was wrong about his motives. He wasn't interested in her money.

But she was right about one thing. His motives weren't pristine.

He'd lusted after her from the moment she'd fallen at his feet. And, while he told himself his actions were pure, he'd kept his distance, seeing her only for a short time each day, because he feared what she did to his self-control.

Self-control! Where was that when he'd kissed her half senseless?

His thoughts flew to the grandfather he'd never known, legendary for his loss of control in respect of one single woman. But this wasn't the same. Raif's was a passing attraction, made more intense by proximity and the dramatic circumstances. He wouldn't let it destroy him.

Yet Tara was right to be suspicious. Right to wonder

if he wanted to seduce her. Not because he was after her inheritance but because he wanted *her*.

Even now, he felt that tell-tale quiver of heat in his groin, legacy of their kiss and the feel of her sweet body clamped against him.

Raif inhaled deeply, trying to find his equilibrium, but only succeeded in drawing in her rose and cinnamon scent. It was rich, earthy, yet elegant. Like the woman herself.

He hadn't been thinking when he kissed her. Or at least, thinking only with his body, not his brain. His twin needs, to silence her and to taste her, had eradicated sensible thought.

That was why he'd let her subsequent doubts get under his skin. She'd grazed his pride and he'd been so unsettled by that embrace he'd reacted in anger.

But the sight of those bruises brought reality back with a vengeance. The ugly marks reinforced her vulnerability.

If ever he needed to be the man he prided himself on being—honourable, honest, a champion of the weak—it was now.

'I'm sorry, Tara. That should never have happened. Either my touch on your arm or the kiss.'

He paused, wondering how best to explain without revealing how close to the edge of sanity she drove him. He couldn't share the complete truth, that she tempted him too much.

He met her questioning gaze. 'I was angry that you doubted me but that doesn't excuse what I did.' He set his shoulders back. 'It won't happen again.'

As he said it, the taste of her lingered in his mouth,

rich, ripe and intoxicating. Denying himself another taste was tantamount to torture. But so be it.

She watched him gravely. Did her straight shoulders drop a little at his words?

'I'm sorry too. I leapt to conclusions. I shouldn't have accused you the way I did.' She drew a breath that seemed to shudder right through her. 'I know you're not like Fuad.'

Damned by faint praise!

But after what had just happened, Raif would take what he could get.

'Thank you.' He paused then forced the words out. 'I'm not used to being questioned. Or having my intentions doubted.' He shook his head. 'I'm used to speaking and being instantly obeyed. And believed. When you thought I was scheming—'

'You don't have to explain. I provoked you.' She spread her hands wide, 'Like you provoked me.'

Raif nodded. 'Neither of us acted well. Can we agree to draw a line under this and move on?'

'Yes. Of course.' She met his eyes then looked away and it struck him that that she seemed diminished. By regret over her actions or worry about the future?

'Excellent.'

It wasn't excellent. It was a damned shame. Because despite his apology, he wasn't sorry about that kiss. The kiss was something he wanted to repeat.

Raif bit back a sigh. It struck him that if he'd ever needed a lesson in humility, and not becoming too prideful, Tara Michaels was the woman to provide it.

'Will you come with me now?' He gestured for her to precede him.

Was that a flicker of doubt in her expression? Then she nodded and Raif felt a surge of pleasure that she trusted him, this far at least.

CHAPTER SIX

As THEY DESCENDED deep into the living rock beneath the citadel, the woman beside Raif grew tense.

In other circumstances he'd be tempted to touch her hand, reassure her. Except he'd just learned how dangerous it was to touch Tara Michaels. He wasn't foolish enough to do it again.

'What's down here?' She sounded far more tentative than moments ago when she'd fired up at him.

Did she think he was leading her to a private dungeon?

'Storage vaults. My ancestors kept grain supplies as protection against famine. There's also a well and massive water cistern. The palace was built to withstand siege.'

'No dungeons?'

He'd been right. She *was* nervous.

'No dungeons.' He didn't explain that his ancestors had believed in swift justice, rather than locking up prisoners for years. That wouldn't reassure her.

'Here we are.' He stopped before a steel door and Tara's eyes widened. The contrast between old stone walls and high-tech security was stark. After completing the security authentications he stood back as the door swung open. Lights flicked on inside.

'After you.'

Tara shot him a doubtful look, then entered.

She took only a couple of steps then stopped, her breath an audible hiss. She turned to take in the display cases all around the room. 'These can't all be real.'

'They are. Every one.' Raif put the tips of his fingers to her back, gently urging her further inside, feeling again that abrupt zing of energy through his body from that point of contact.

If anything were needed to remind him to keep his distance, that did it.

And the heavy craving deep inside. A craving for one more taste, one touch.

Raif stepped to one side, distancing himself. Yet her tantalising fragrance lingered in his nostrils.

'These are incredible!' Glowing green eyes held his, then she turned to study a nearby display. Its centrepiece was a curved dagger in a gold scabbard, studded with precious gems. The hilt was of gold surrounding one of the biggest faceted emeralds the world had ever seen.

Her eyes rounded. The royal jewels had that effect.

Raif watched her move from the dagger to a solid gold platter, its rim studded with precious cabochon rubies, then to a small casket decorated with diamonds.

Now she bent over another case, her gaze intent. Raif moved closer, curious to see what held her so rapt.

'Look at the workmanship. Isn't it amazing?'

Of all the riches in the cabinet it was the smallest, a bangle studded with small stones the colour of cranberries.

'See the gold work? The intricate beading and the exquisite forms?'

Raif leaned closer, drawn by her excitement and assurance as she described the methods some long-ago goldsmith had used to create the decoration of tiny birds and flowers.

'And the stones?'

'Spinels. Don't they have a fabulous colour?' But once again she was exclaiming over the fine workmanship.

It fascinated him that she was drawn by the craftsmanship, not how expensive the piece, or how bright the gems. Usually visitors stared at the biggest, most glittering pieces. Some didn't make it past the emerald dagger.

Then he remembered a detail from the report he'd received on Tara Michaels. She worked as a sales assistant in an exclusive jewellery store. Raif had thought of her as merely a smiling face at a cash register. Now he realised his mistake.

He'd underestimated her. Again.

The idea discomfited him.

Upstairs he'd taken out his frustrations on her, kissing her, only to discover Tara wasn't a woman to be so easily silenced. She'd stood up to him as few people did. Even if her doubts about him weren't correct, she'd been right to wonder about his intentions.

He should have known not to expect her to be predictable. Tara Michaels was many things, including a problem of increasing proportions, but predictable wasn't one of them.

'You have a real interest in these.'

She looked up, surprised. 'Who wouldn't? They're unique. This is an extraordinary collection.'

Raif nodded. She wasn't the first to say so. He'd been urged to have the treasury inventory updated and permit the public display of some pieces. But it wasn't high on his list of priorities.

Now, though, an idea began to form.

Tara made a sweeping gesture with one hand. 'I feel privileged to see this, but why—?'

'Why bring you here?' It had seemed a good idea. Now Raif felt the gesture was too crudely obvious. Too much like bragging. 'To prove I'm not after your inheritance. My nation is rich and my personal wealth significant. I thought seeing this would convince you.'

Of course he wasn't scheming to get her inheritance.

She'd known it almost as soon as she'd accused him. But she'd been so upset after what happened in the throne room, and by Raif's repudiation after their kiss, she hadn't been thinking straight.

Tara's gaze drifted across the vast room lined with priceless treasures. No wonder he'd been insulted at her accusation. Her cousin Fuad might be hungry for money, but not so the Sheikh of Nahrat.

She felt foolish.

'I apologise. It was a crazy idea, I know.' She focused on his chin, rather than meet those intense eyes that she found so worryingly attractive. 'I shouldn't—'

'Of course you should.' His words jerked her gaze up. This time Tara felt a little judder of delight as their eyes locked. 'You've learned your family is trying to exploit you. If you don't stand up for yourself, who will?'

Raif paused and then, remarkably, his mouth rucked

up in a hint of a smile that did devastating things to Tara. Warmth trailed through her, eddying lower and lower to places she didn't want to think about.

'I applaud you for standing up for yourself.'

'You do? That wasn't the impression you gave.'

He inclined his head, a groove dimpling his cheek as his smile grew wry. 'I overreacted. It's rare for anyone to take me to task, or question my judgement. No one else does except my aunt.'

'I'd like to meet your aunt.' The words escaped before Tara had a chance to think better of them.

Instead of annoying him, the comment made his smile grow. And with it that fluttery feeling inside her.

'She'll enjoy meeting you too. She's in the US, visiting friends. It was her carpet you stowed away in.'

'I see.' Tara wasn't sure what to say. The mention of her unorthodox arrival brought heat to her cheeks. Then there was Raif's implication that she'd be here when his aunt returned.

Once more he seemed to read her thoughts. 'I'm afraid that for your safety your stay here will be extended. Now Fuad knows your location he'll set people watching in case you leave.'

Tara nodded, repressing a shudder.

'But there's an upside.'

'There is?' She couldn't see one. She was still a prisoner, even if in a gilded, beautiful palace.

'Of course. You said you feel restless after being cooped up. How would you like to be my guest at a dinner tonight?'

Attending a royal event was nerve-racking. Especially as Tara was busy fretting over Fuad's next move. His ambassador must have reported back by now. But at least, compared with her cousin's bullying behaviour, a royal dinner shouldn't be too daunting.

Tara smoothed her hands down her dress and told herself she had no reason to be nervous. They were just people, even if they were the sort who frequented royal dinners. She'd never attended such an event. Her visits to Dhalkur had always been as a private citizen.

She pivoted before the mirror, pleased that she'd stand up to scrutiny thanks to the stunning clothes Raif had provided.

The sapphire-blue dress draped her curves, cinching in at her waist and flaring in a flirtatious ripple around her legs. Tara loved it. It was what she would have chosen if she had an unlimited budget. She'd never worn haute couture but knew this cobweb-fine silk with hand-sewn detailing around the deep V neckline was expensive.

What would Raif think when he saw her?

That shouldn't matter, and yet…

This morning he'd kissed her till her head spun and her senses sang. The memory made the fine hairs on her arms stand up and her insides quiver. She'd been with him every step of the way. Resisting had never entered her head.

He'd acted out of temper but she'd felt, or thought she'd felt, his body stir against hers. As if it wasn't just annoyance he experienced or the need to impose his will. Afterwards he'd disarmed her with his apology and wry confession that he wasn't used to being crossed.

That had only made him more attractive.

Too attractive.

He confused her. Tara wanted to trust him, and so far it seemed she had every reason to. Yet, despite her profound attraction, she couldn't quite accept he had no ulterior motive. There was something, some secret he kept from her. Or did her situation make her paranoid?

He had ultimate power and she had none. That, above all, made her nervous. The feeling of powerlessness evoked panic.

She was a refugee, dependent on his charity till she found safety elsewhere. Despite her family connections, she wasn't royal. She'd never been inducted into that exclusive clique. She'd grown up with two wonderful parents who loved her and the chance to live in some fascinating places. They'd had enough money to live comfortably but they weren't rich or powerful.

A knock on the door sounded.

'Coming!' Tara slipped on her sapphire-blue shoes. When she straightened the door was open, revealing Raif's tall frame.

Tara's breath seized. She swallowed, her mouth suddenly dry. She told herself not to be silly, but her body had other ideas. Her nipples peaked as if vying for his attention and low in her belly that needy sensation was back.

He looked stunning in made-to-measure formal clothes. She recalled the strength of his arms lashing her to him and the taste of his firm mouth as he bent her to him and she went up in flames. Even the texture of his hair against her fingertips had been incredibly erotic.

'Raif.' Her voice was a betraying wisp of sound. 'I wasn't expecting you.'

He strolled across the room towards her, his movements easy with fluid grace.

Another little shimmy of excitement started up inside. Was there anything about this man that didn't appeal?

Yes. His determination to have his own way.

'I thought you'd like an escort. You don't know the other guests. I'll introduce you to make it a little easier.'

Easier! Walking in to a royal dinner with the Sheikh? She'd hoped to slip in quietly and not draw attention.

'That's very kind. Thank you.'

A faint smile curved his lips as if her words pleased him. 'Shall we?' He gestured to the door then stepped back, as if not wanting to crowd her.

Or not wanting to touch her. Despite her determination to be cautious with him, the thought jarred.

As they turned down a wide corridor decorated with beautiful murals, Raif kept his distance. A message that he had no intention of repeating their kiss?

She already knew that. Yet disappointment took root.

What had she expected? That he'd see her in her finery, sophisticated and even a little sexy, and be smitten?

The rhythm of her high heels clicking on marble faltered as she realised that was exactly it.

She wanted Raif to be smitten.

Wanted him to admire her. Not see her as a problem or an annoyance.

She wanted him to regret rejecting her.

Fool. Fool. Fool.

This was dangerous.

'Tara, are you okay?' Warmth teased her as his fingers gripped her elbow. Her sleeve was no protection against his heat, or the shimmery wave of longing radiating from his touch.

'Fine, thanks.' She pasted on a smile and looked up at him. Her heart gave a mighty thump that confirmed her misgivings.

She was too old for a crush on the man who'd saved her. This was something different.

Raif was so close she could lean in to rest her head against his chest.

Being short, she'd spent most of her life proving she was perfectly able to look after herself and defying those who equated her lack of height with a need for them to make decisions for her.

Strange that now, looking up into Raif's gleaming gaze, acutely aware of the latent power in his tall frame, all Tara felt was the desire to burrow closer.

As if being pressed against his big body would be the most wonderful thing in the world. The disparity in height didn't make her defensive, ready to reject a casually patronising attitude. Instead, his powerful body beckoned.

Tara swallowed hard, inhaling the faintest drift of sandalwood.

She wanted to surrender to those forces he'd unleashed a few hours ago.

'New shoes,' she murmured, to explain her stumble. Then wished she hadn't when Raif, still holding her, looked down. Tara felt supremely aware of his scrutiny. Did he like the way the high-heeled shoes enhanced the curve of her calves and made her legs look longer?

'Very pretty.'

She could *not* feel his gaze drifting up her legs. Yet her skin tingled as if from a caress.

'Thank you.' Quickly changing the subject, she found herself promising once again to repay him for the clothes.

Gravely he heard her out then said merely, 'If it pleases you to do so, of course. But it's my pleasure, especially as I get to enjoy seeing you look so lovely.'

Tara opened her mouth then shut it. She couldn't object because he'd left it up to her to decide whether to pay him back. As for the comment about how good she looked, she'd seem churlish to object to that. It wasn't Raif's fault she felt self-conscious.

'Shall we go?' He stepped close again, leading her through the palace. 'There will be some guests tonight that I think you'll find interesting.'

By the time they reached the public rooms Tara was looking forward to meeting the people he'd described. Until a footman opened a door and they stepped into a long chamber that took her breath away.

The vaulted ceiling was midnight-blue, dusted with sparkling stars that she discovered later were white sapphires. The walls were a muted gold, decorated at the base with mosaics of lilies that looked almost real. A long, elaborately set table extended down the room, and at this end stood a crowd of beautifully dressed guests, all watching her.

Every head bowed. The men inclining from the waist and the women curtseying, making Tara shockingly aware that she had her hand tucked through the Sheikh's elbow.

People did not touch a sheikh, especially in public.

She moved to withdraw her hand, but Raif forestalled her, his other hand covering hers.

Fortunately the guests were too polite to reveal shock, but as she and Raif circulated there were lots of curious glances. Clearly her presence caused a stir. Because she was from Dhalkur, or because he escorted her?

Raif introduced her as niece to the Sheikh of Dhalkur, here on a personal visit. That was nicely vague and made her sound like the sort of person who might belong at a royal event.

Instead of an intruder.

She shivered as Raif escorted her to her place at the table then excused himself, saying protocol dictated he sit with representatives from another kingdom.

Tara told herself she was relieved not to spend the evening with him. Yet she felt a jangle of disappointment, watching him go to the head of the table, stopping along the way to speak to more guests. A couple of beautiful, sloe-eyed women hung on his every word, their smiles too inviting for Tara's liking.

'He's very impressive, isn't he?' She turned to find an auburn-haired man smiling at her, his accent familiar from time she'd spent in Australia.

'Impressive?' She pretended to ponder.

'Our host. Urbane and sociable, but with a mind like a steel trap when it comes to business.'

'And what is your business, Mr...?'

'Fletcher. Steve Fletcher. I'm a geologist. And you're—?'

'Tara Michaels. Passing through before heading back to London.'

She read a glint of appreciation in his eyes. 'But

here long enough to share dinner.' He gestured to the table where their names were inscribed on neighbouring place cards. 'The evening is looking up already.'

Tara laughed. She'd forgotten how upfront Australians could be.

As the evening progressed, her neighbours proved friendly and fascinating. On her other side was a woman with a warm chuckle and an infectious sense of humour who headed a medical research team. Across the table was a curator from the national museum whose specialty was old jewellery, and his wife, a teacher of English, eager to practise her language skills.

How long since she'd simply enjoyed chatting with others?

Through the last stages of her mother's illness and in the dark weeks that followed, she'd been absorbed in grief. Then had come the trauma of imprisonment in her uncle's palace. No wonder she revelled in her new acquaintances.

As for her brighter than usual smiles, they weren't about proving to herself that she didn't miss Raif. Or hurt reaction to his grim expression whenever she found him watching her.

Had she offended him in some way, breaking some royal protocol?

Tara firmed her jaw. If so, maybe she wouldn't be allowed out in public again. She intended to make the most of it. Ignoring Raif's dark stare, she turned to the man beside her.

CHAPTER SEVEN

THE EVENING TESTED Raif's patience to the limit.

It had begun badly when Fuad had phoned, something he'd never done before. Ostensibly the call had been about the old Sheikh's declining health, but soon he'd moved to increasingly shrill demands that Raif send Tara back.

The man sounded obsessed. Or perhaps simply desperate. Raif had heard the Dhalkuri Royal Council wasn't all in favour of Fuad taking the throne, so he was probably grasping at any way to shore up his position.

Raif had barely hung on to his temper during the call. He'd finally ended it by saying Tara was here as his most *personal* guest, leaving Fuad to splutter indignantly over what that might imply. The conversation had left him seething and even more determined to support her.

Since then Raif had spent the evening watching his most conservative guests struggle to hide their affront that he'd personally escorted a single woman to dinner, something he'd never done before. And not just any woman, but a Dhalkuri!

On top of that he had to watch Tara smile at that too-attentive Australian.

Pain circled Raif's jaw and he forced himself to relax and unclench his teeth.

He'd asked his secretary to ensure she was seated near the museum curator, given their shared interest in old jewellery. The Australian he hadn't met, but, given his senior role in a mining company, Raif had imagined someone older.

Not a young man who leaned too close to Tara. Who made her laugh that low, throaty laugh that Raif felt like the drag of velvet across his skin.

Raif wanted Tara to laugh like that with him, not some upstart Australian.

He wanted her smiles for himself.

Raif's fingers tightened into a fist and he had to focus on relaxing them. On smoothing his frown.

How could he be distracted by one tiny woman? One at the centre of a diplomatic furore that Raif really didn't need.

Yes, she was vivacious.

And unbelievably sexy.

And annoying.

And stronger than she looked.

Touching her today—okay, more than touching— had unleashed forces Raif usually kept well under control.

He was profoundly disturbed to discover his control of his libido had slipped again.

Raif's control had never slipped before Tara Michaels tumbled into his world.

He'd been provoked into kissing her but he'd pulled

back. Because she was under his protection. And because Raif didn't do unbridled passion. Ever.

This hot surge of feeling was new and distracting.

The Australian pulled out her chair as everyone rose from the table and Raif wanted to shove him away from her.

For a moment he toyed with the notion that it was jealousy he felt, but dismissed it. He was never jealous.

He'd never needed to be. As the only child of loving, if strict, parents, he'd had a charmed life. Until his early teens when they'd died and he'd inherited the sheikhdom. But he'd had sound advisors to ease him into his new role. Everything he'd ever wanted had been within his grasp.

As for wanting Tara, that was natural. She was attractive and intriguing. He'd wanted women before. The difference was that this time he couldn't have her. *That* was why his response seemed so intense.

Farewelling his guests, Raif managed to keep his gaze off Tara till finally it was time to join her.

'Ms Michaels.' He resorted to formality for the sake of those around them.

'Your Majesty. What a lovely evening.' Her smile hit him square in the chest.

Still the Australian lingered. 'Your Majesty,' he said. 'Thank you for tonight's dinner. It's been an honour and a pleasure.'

Raif inclined his head. 'You're welcome, Mr Fletcher. I hear you're to begin work in the outer provinces.'

'Not straight away.' His gaze flicked to Tara. 'I thought I'd stay in the city and see the sights first.'

'Really?' Raif frowned. 'I understood from your CEO that he expected you on the ground immediately.'

The enterprise was in part funded by the crown. It might be timely to ensure an early start to the geological survey, as originally planned.

As the chamberlain ushered the last guests out Raif was surprised at the satisfaction he felt, watching the ruddy-haired Australian go while Tara remained here, at his side.

Possessive as well as jealous?

He couldn't be.

Raif was simply pleased she was here where he could protect her.

He'd never allow Fuad to get his hands on Tara.

Or the Australian?

'You enjoyed yourself?' he asked, leading Tara away.

Her smile widened and Raif dismissed the Australian from his thoughts.

'It was lovely. Thank you. Just what I needed. It was terrific to meet such interesting people.' She shrugged. 'I'm a bit of a people person and I've spent too much time alone with my thoughts.'

'I'm pleased you had a good time. It must be a relief that you don't have to hide from public view anymore.'

Though, judging by Fuad's reaction tonight, her presence here would fuel more trouble. And the backlash wouldn't just be from across the border.

Already there'd been talk about what Tara was doing, alone and unchaperoned in the palace. About what his relationship was with a woman from the Dhalkuri royal family.

As Dhalkur and Nahrat were traditional enemies,

and many believed that shouldn't change, Raif had to tread carefully.

He hadn't been careful when he'd entered the banqueting hall with her hand on his arm.

Raif had acted deliberately, defying anyone to express disapproval. Knowing his action would eventually be reported to Fuad. He was determined to signal that Tara was under his protection. Everyone, Fuad and his representatives, as well as Nahratis who might take issue with her presence, needed to know that.

Raif had crossed a boundary when he gave her sanctuary and had no intention of going back on his word now. No matter the repercussions. Only his support kept her free. It was what any decent man would do. It was *not* a sign of personal weakness.

'Here.' He opened a door and ushered her inside a sitting room.

'I thought you were taking me to my room?' Was that disappointment in her voice?

Did she want him in her private suite? His brain snagged on the notion, till he told himself not to be distracted.

Nevertheless, his gaze caught on her as she moved to take the seat he indicated. She was poised and sexy in those high heels that turned her gait into a sensuous sway. The subtle sheen of blue fabric shimmered across her breasts and hips.

Raif swallowed, his throat sandpaper dry.

He'd given orders that she be provided with a wardrobe suitable for a princess. It would have been easier if his orders hadn't been followed so assiduously.

Easier but much less enjoyable.

Besides, it wasn't her clothes. Alone of all the

women tonight, Tara wore no jewellery, and if she wore make-up he couldn't see it. Yet the golden glow of her skin, her fine eyes and glossy dark hair with its hint of mahogany red were embellishment enough.

She'd look good in anything.

Or nothing.

Raif took a seat opposite, corralling his thoughts. 'We have things to discuss.' He wouldn't tell her about Fuad's call, though. That would just worry her.

She sat demurely, hands in her lap. Raif's gaze dipped to her mouth, dark pink and lush, then back to her questioning eyes.

'Now it's public knowledge you're here, you can have more freedom.'

He'd thought her eyes pretty before. Now they turned bright as polished gems. He'd pleased her. Stoically he squashed thoughts of other, more personal ways he might please her.

'That's wonderful!'

'You'll still have to be careful. No dashing into the city unescorted.'

Because her cousin was desperate and underhanded enough to have thugs waiting for a chance to grab her. Nor could Raif completely discount the possibility that one of his own people might assist, believing it inappropriate that their Sheikh associate with a woman whose family was seen by some die-hards as the enemy.

'You think Fuad would snatch me off the street?' Her eyes rounded.

'You know him better than I do. What do you think?'

'I wouldn't put anything past him.' She chewed her lip. 'So what did you have in mind?'

'Two things. You met the jewellery curator from the national museum tonight. It looked like you got on well.'

'We did. He and his wife are charming and his work is so fascinating.'

'I'm glad you think so. He's persuaded me to up-date the inventory of royal jewels. You can assist him.'

'Me?' Her brow pinched. 'I'm no jeweller. I don't have formal qualifications.'

'You have a good eye and a real appreciation.'

She shook her head. 'An appreciation, yes. I've picked up a bit over the years, but I'm not an expert.'

'I'm not looking for expertise—the curator will pro-vide that. I thought it would appeal to you.' Though it was, now he thought about it, unpaid work. 'If you're not interested—'

'Oh, I'm interested! If you think I can really help, it would be wonderful.'

Raif nodded, pleased his plan was so well-received. 'It will mainly be a matter of taking notes, and, know-ing the curator, listening to his thoughts on the history of each piece.'

A smile tugged her lips and it struck him again that Tara was a woman who didn't need adornment to be attractive. That smile alone would entice any man. Awareness shivered low in his belly.

'I'd like nothing better! If you're sure he wants me. He doesn't already have an assistant?'

'His assistant will be busy at the museum.' Raif's old friend was thrilled to be given the go-ahead for the project and if it kept Tara occupied so she didn't feel isolated… 'So, that's sorted. My staff will arrange a meeting.'

'You said there were two things.'

Raif nodded. This next was trickier. Not for her, but for him. Yet he had no intention of bowing to Fuad or any diehards who held a grudge against Dhalkur. It was time for change.

'I'd like you to come on my visits around the capital and later to a provincial centre.'

Her eyes flashed to his and he read her excitement. 'I'd love to get out. What would I have to do?'

Raif told himself that wasn't elation he felt at her excitement. She chafed at staying here, that was all. How different she was to the women he knew who'd enjoy relaxing in luxury, waited on hand and foot.

'You'll see the sights, attend a few receptions, meet some locals. You won't have a formal role, but you'd participate in any welcome festivities.'

'I can do that.' But now her smile suddenly crimped tight. 'Thank you. You're very kind, very…thoughtful. I've put you to a lot of trouble.'

'Tara?' Was it a trick of the light or did her eyes shine over-bright?

She looked down, restlessly smoothing the shimmery fabric of her skirt.

He wanted to take her hands. The woman he'd come to admire was feisty and determined, sometimes too much so. He didn't like this glimpse of what looked like sadness.

'I thought you'd be happy to get out of the palace.'

Tara swallowed, feeling the lump of scalding emotion in her throat. Stupid to be upset now when nothing was wrong.

It was his kindness that undid her. The reminder that, uninvited guest though she was, Raif tried to make her stay pleasant. She still couldn't believe he was allowing her the chance to work with an expert cataloguing those exquisite treasures. But it was the idea of getting outdoors again, away from the confinement of four walls that most affected her.

She blinked, forcing back the prickle of tears.

It had been the same when her cousin Salim had contacted her on her mother's death, asking what she needed, what he could do to help. His thoughtfulness had threatened to undo her then. As Raif's did now.

She'd been through so much her emotions were shot.

'I am happy. I'm thrilled.' She pasted on a smile that she hoped reflected excitement, though her facial muscles felt too tight. 'With all your other responsibilities I'm amazed you have time to think of me. I can't tell you how much I appreciate it.'

Raif's forehead knotted and he waved a dismissive hand. 'It's nothing. Others will make the arrangements.'

Yet it was only because of his intervention that she wasn't at Fuad's mercy. And Raif had gone further. He turned her stay into something other than another incarceration. Tara felt guilty that she'd doubted him, wondering if he was like Fuad, aiming to grab her fortune.

Her ribs tightened around her fast-beating heart.

Raif made her feel so much. He had an uncanny ability to rub her up the wrong way and bring her to bristling, uncharacteristic antagonism. Yet despite his arrogance and her occasional doubts he was kind, considerate and far too appealing. He made her feel scary, unfamiliar yearnings.

Tara shot to her feet, afraid of where her thoughts might lead.

When Raif had invited her to join him after dinner she'd wondered if he was going to kiss her again. She'd been on tenterhooks, wondering if he'd take her to his suite.

Instead he really did want to *talk*.

It wasn't talk she wanted from him.

If she stayed much longer there was a chance she'd reveal that. Her pride couldn't take another rejection.

'Thank you, Raif.' She paused as he rose to tower above her. She only had to take a couple of steps to close the space between them. A couple of steps and she could put her hand on that sturdy chest, feel his heartbeat, smell his heat and sandalwood spice scent. Reach up and cup his jaw. Pull his head down for another kiss. 'I'd better go.'

'Are you all right?' Concern laced his tone, roughening it deliciously as he stepped nearer.

Tara shivered as her body reacted. She arched her neck back to hold his gaze. His eyes gleamed brighter than ever, obsidian-black. Yet to her fevered mind his gaze looked soft, not hard. Beckoning, not distant.

She swallowed again, nostrils flaring as she inhaled his unique male scent.

'I'm fine.' Her fingers flexed and she realised with a jolt that she was imagining dragging her hand across the dark olive skin of his cheek. Down to the sharp line of his jaw. Would his skin feel rough there? Her palm prickled as if tickled by imaginary stubble.

Tara whipped her hands behind her back, like a child caught reaching for forbidden goodies.

'I'm just very tired.'

That was such a lie. She was wired. She wouldn't sleep for hours.

His eyes widened infinitesimally.

Did he guess she lied?

Could he sense the current of awareness passing through her? It hummed in her veins and across her skin, drawing her nipples into tight buds and making her far too aware of that hollow, needy sensation deep inside.

Tara licked suddenly dry lips then forgot to breathe as Raif followed the movement of her tongue.

A heavy whump of sensation punched through her. She canted towards him, drawn by his magnetism.

His eyes glowed and his nostrils arched as if he scented her arousal in the thickening air.

One second more. One move…

With a rush of blood to her head Tara pulled back, stunned that she still had the power to. She swallowed, regret lodging hard against her breastbone as she conjured the words she needed.

'Thanks again, Raif.' Her voice thickened on his name and the taste of it almost undid her resolve. As did the fire in those burning eyes. 'It's time I turned in. Goodnight.'

She swung away, movements clumsy, feet leaden, and walked to the door.

Every step she waited for his voice calling her back, or the touch of his hand on her shoulder, pulling her against him. Confirming that she wasn't alone in this. That he too felt this…yearning.

Instead, with her hand on the door, she heard, 'Goodnight, Tara. Sleep well.'

Her mouth trembled but she kept her head high. No matter what, she'd vanquish her attraction to Raif. She *would*.

CHAPTER EIGHT

THE NEXT FIVE days sped by. Tara met Raif daily but he never hinted at anything like intimacy by word or look.

She found that deflating, even though she'd decided she had to conquer her attraction. Surely something that affected her so suddenly couldn't last?

Yet Tara enjoyed the companionable time with him. It made her feel calm and grounded, which was baffling because she'd never needed anyone else to help her do that.

Each day she went out with the Sheikh's entourage. She had no official role but Raif always took time to tell her about each venue and introduce her. It was so fascinating that she managed not to mind the curiosity she provoked.

Her favourite excursion was to the old covered markets, inspecting building improvements. For Tara it was a chance to enjoy the vast array of goods on sale, from carpets, brass and copper wear, leather goods and silks to huge mounds of vibrantly coloured spices and fruit.

As well, each day she spent hours in the royal treasury. She'd been nervous at first, conscious of her lack of formal qualifications. But to her delight she found herself up to the job. Sometimes she even noticed things her new colleague missed. Like identifying the design work around some emeralds as South American, thanks to her years living there. That led to a new line of investigation on the source of the piece.

It made her think of reviving her idea of getting formal qualifications. She'd put that on hold when her father died and she'd moved with her mother to England, and again when her mother became ill.

Lulled by the rocking motion of the four-wheel drive crossing the desert, Tara was musing on that when they reached the summit of a huge sand dune and stopped. Her breath caught at the scene below her.

All around were shades of ochre and gold, and above, the bright blue of the sky. Before them, between the dune and a rocky cliff, lay a miniature forest of green. Tall, graceful palms towered over other, shrubbier trees and she caught the tantalising glint of water.

'An oasis!' Thrilled, she turned to see Raif in the driver's seat, watching her.

Tara's ease shattered as her pulse quickened. There was something about his gleaming eyes that made her insides flutter.

'You like it?' Raif's voice burred softly, making her pulse thrum an unfamiliar beat.

Tara yanked her head back to the view.

'It's amazing. I've never seen anything like it. The change from barren sand to lush greenery is so sudden.'

Was she babbling? Suddenly Tara felt self-conscious. Surely she imagined the change in his expression. Just because she found him fascinating didn't mean he felt the same. He'd been nothing but a perfect host for days.

How disappointing she'd found that!

The sun glinted off the vehicles that had gone ahead. 'Are those tents I see?'

'They are. This is our campsite.'

Surprised, Tara turned back to him. 'I thought we were visiting towns. That we'd stay there.'

'Afraid you'll miss out on amenities?' His mouth flattened. 'Don't worry, you'll find the camp quite comfortable.'

'I didn't mean that. I'm just surprised. I'd love to camp in the desert. I've never done that.'

He held her gaze, then nodded. 'I'm glad to provide a new experience.' He started up the engine and drove downhill, manoeuvring over the treacherous surface with consummate skill. 'The towns are over there.' He nodded towards a distant blue ridge. 'We'll go there later.'

The oasis was fascinating. It had a peaceful quality, enhanced by the fact their accommodation was set away from vehicles and attendants.

Raif led her into a grove sheltered by tall palms where two big tents sat side by side.

Crazy to read anything into the way they were located together. It was just that, unlike the guards and other attendants, she was Raif's private guest.

Nevertheless, Tara was supremely conscious of the man beside her. As always, she felt their disparity in height. But now the difference between them seemed even more pronounced. She was hyper-aware of his athletic body, from his loose-limbed stride to his upright stance and innate air of assurance. Even the easy swing of his arms reminded her of the power in those big hands when he'd held her close and kissed her.

When all she could think of was losing herself in the glorious oblivion of passion.

'I'll leave you to freshen up before lunch.'

Quickly she nodded, not turning to meet his penetrating stare and definitely not trusting her voice to respond evenly.

'Then we'll head out for a site visit.'

In other words, despite the exotic setting, this trip was business. Not a romantic getaway.

Tara swallowed and scraped her voice together. 'I'll look forward to it.'

'See you in half an hour.'

'I'll be ready.'

She felt his stare but pretended to be fascinated by the sprawling tent before her as he strode the few metres to his own, even larger tent, topped by the royal standard that stirred in the breeze.

Taking a deep breath, Tara silently berated herself. Raif's expression when they'd stopped at the top of the sand dune was *not* heavy with desire. Even if it had made her hot all over. As for his regard just now, he probably just wondered why she was so silent.

See? She could be sensible. That was a first step in conquering her awareness of him.

Pushing aside the canvas flap that served as a door, she walked into her desert accommodation.

And stopped short at the sheer Arabian Nights beauty of it.

The tent looked big from the outside but it was larger inside, with a high ceiling that emphasised the sense of space. Rich carpets in jewel hues covered the floor and some of the walls, creating a sense of lush opulence.

Tara was reminded of an ornate jewellery box she'd

catalogued the day before. Of solid gold, it was set with precious and semi-precious stones that created a rainbow of colours. Here, a similar kaleidoscope met the eye, but whoever had decorated this space knew what they were doing. Despite the range of colours, they blended together harmoniously.

The long swathes of filmy material around the bed gave it a rich feel, as did the burnished brass tables and silk cushions covered in exquisite embroidery. There was even a bowl of deeply scented roses on an inlaid wooden chest of drawers.

Shaking her head, Tara took off her shoes, curling her toes into the deep pile of the intricately patterned carpet.

Her mother had been something of an expert on carpets, given that the headquarters of the Royal Guild of Carpet Weavers, established by Tara's grandmother, was next door to the Dhalkuri palace. Tara's mother had been in and out of the place throughout her childhood—hence her friendship with Yunis—and she'd taught her daughter well. This carpet was not only beautiful but also old and very, very precious.

A huff of dry laughter escaped Tara's throat.

This was how Raif went camping?

Had she really thought, even for a second, that he was interested in her paltry fortune?

Her stunned gaze took in the gorgeous space. All it needed was an ornate lamp with a genie to make it the stuff of fantasies.

Or a tall, dark handsome man with hard features and an even harder body…

The thought set her insides shivering again.

On bare feet she crossed the room, discovering a wardrobe complete with a range of her new clothes. Not just the ones she'd chosen for this visit, but also some made of that butterfly-sheer silk, beaded at neck and hem.

The sight of those glamorous, sensuous outfits set up a jangling sensation inside, but she mastered the urge to wonder if they'd been packed for Raif's benefit.

That wasn't going to happen. Despite what some eager maid assumed.

Spying another door, Tara discovered a well-appointed bathroom complete with fluffy towels and a range of toiletries. Another vase sat on a bench top, this time filled with scented gardenias.

Tara was stunned by the level of luxury. She knew Raif had grown up in enormous wealth, but he seemed a man who didn't need opulence to be happy. The vehicle he'd driven today had been serviceable rather than luxurious and his clothes, though well-made, weren't ostentatious.

Were there sybaritic touches in his accommodation too? Or was his personal space more restrained? Had he specifically asked his staff to create this amazing bower for her? More likely a helpful staffer had pulled out all the stops for His Majesty's guest.

Or perhaps Raif brought his lovers to this beautiful place. Maybe these furnishings were used whenever he wanted a discreet love nest for his latest amour.

Pain jabbed between Tara's ribs.

Nose wrinkling at the direction of her thoughts, she washed her face and hands, then let down her hair and brushed it before arranging it high in a severe knot. Ignoring the delicious silks in the wardrobe, she located a cool cotton dress and low sandals.

She'd give no one reason to believe she was here as Raif's lover.

* * *

For once Raif had trouble concentrating. Usually nothing distracted him from his job.

Right now, that job was listening to the elders of the town where a new solar energy farm had been established. Yet as they discussed changes in the region, job opportunities and the impact of newcomers moving into town, Raif's attention wandered.

To Tara, of course.

He'd organised the oasis stay because it was one of his favourite places, where he went to unwind. He'd thought its natural beauty would soothe Tara in this difficult time and when she'd first seen it, it seemed he'd been right.

Delight jolted adrenaline into his blood when he'd seen her wide stare and stunned smile. But doubts crowded at her reaction when she learned they were to stay the night. Perhaps camping, even with every possible luxury, wasn't her style. Perhaps, after all, she didn't appreciate the peace and majesty of the place as he did.

Strange how that had felt like a personal blow. He'd felt rebuffed, sharing a place that was special to him, only to face her lukewarm enthusiasm.

He'd gone out of his way to make her accommodation special. As if his staff couldn't be trusted to provide what was necessary.

As if he wanted her to fall for the place, to appreciate it as he did.

To appreciate him?

Raif wasn't so needy.

With an effort he dragged his attention back to the current discussion. Two elders with differing opinions debated between themselves. Time to rein them in and turn the discussion in a more constructive direction.

'Sir!'

The head of his close personal protection team approached and Raif frowned. Despite his professionally schooled features, Raif read the man's tension.

'A word, sir. Urgently.'

All heads turned and the debate petered into silence.

Raif rose. 'Excuse me a moment.' He found it hard to believe there was a threat. His people were loyal.

'There's trouble at the community centre, sir.' Once outside, his bodyguard slanted a look across the square to the building where Tara was taking tea with the local women.

Raif's heart stumbled to a halt then accelerated into a rackety beat.

'Tell me.' His fingers closed around the guard's arm. All was quiet. Too quiet?

'A young woman with a baby slipped out from a back room. She reported armed men in the building. Strangers, with a different accent. She thinks from Dhalkur.'

The hairs at the back of Raif's neck stood up.

Were they here for Tara? It should be impossible but it was the only reasonable explanation. They were fifty kilometres from the border. Even Fuad would be wary of an armed incursion into sovereign territory. Which meant it likely the men were a rogue group, easily denied by Fuad if something went wrong. And likely more dangerous than trained soldiers. Raif's heart plummeted.

'You believe her? It's not some story?'

'No, one of my men saw an armed gunman attempting to slip out. He had a woman with him. We believe it was Ms Michaels. When he saw my man he shouted an order over his shoulder and withdrew. Now the entrance is locked from the inside. We've heard male voices and women crying.'

Raif made to cross the square, but the bodyguard stepped in front of him.

'Please, sir. You need to leave this to us.'

'What do you have in mind? Storming the building? With scores of hostages in there?'

He shook his head, his brain conjuring and rejecting one scenario after another. Armed intervention could end in a bloodbath.

'How many men?'

'We've identified only two voices.'

Vaguely, Raif was aware of his quickened breathing, his hurried pulse. There was a sick feeling in his gut as he thought of vulnerable women, held by gunmen. Of Tara. His heart lurched. He'd promised her protection. Yet he'd brought her into danger.

As Sheikh, he had a responsibility to all his people trapped in there and to their families.

As a man it was the thought of Tara that filled his mind and iced his veins with fear.

Tara stood, hands bound, watching the two armed men. Fear was a harsh, metallic taste on her tongue and her pulse raced ten to the dozen.

A quick glance over her shoulder revealed all the women standing, silent, behind her, their expressions a mixture of fear and defiance. A couple of them had protested when the men had bound Tara's hands and tried to hustle her out of the building. They'd been struck down with vicious blows, but now their quiet sobs had stopped.

Guilt sat heavy in Tara's chest. She'd brought this horror on these friendly women. These men were Dhalkuris and it was her they wanted.

Her senses strained to heightened awareness as terror dragged every muscle tight.

Fuad wanted her alive. But if something went wrong, as it now appeared, would they dispose of any witnesses? The men looked panicked. Panicked men made mistakes, which could work in her favour, or ramp up the danger.

Better they take her, than endanger all these people. If she offered herself as a willing hostage, surely whoever was outside would let them pass. She'd be delivering herself into Fuad's hands but there was no other option.

Tara stepped forward. 'I'll come with you quietly if you let the others go. The guards will let you pass if I'm with you.'

She slammed to a halt as a woven hanging on a far wall lifted. Her eyes widened. It took a moment to realise what she saw wasn't the wall breaking, but someone entering through a door hidden by the traditional weaving.

There was a shout, the gunmen swivelling. Then Tara's heart stood still as Raif stepped into the room.

Relief filled her, till she saw those ugly weapons pointed at him, and her knees went to jelly.

He said nothing, nor did he look at her after one sweeping survey of the large room. Instead he lifted his arms from his sides and slowly turned on the spot. His movements were measured, confident even, and his austere expression revealed no fear. His regal bearing, as much as his snowy robe and head scarf, put him in a different category to the two men before him, dusty and nervous-looking despite their weapons.

'Don't come any closer,' one of the men said, his voice grim.

'I'm unarmed.' Raif's voice rang through the strained silence with the authority of total assurance. 'I come in peace to discover why you're threatening my people.'

One of the intruders whispered something to his companion. The other shook his head, then growled, 'We're here for the woman.' He jerked his head towards Tara. 'We have no interest in the others. Let us pass and no one will be hurt.'

'She doesn't want to go with you.'

'It doesn't matter what she wants. She belongs in Dhalkur. Our orders are—' He broke off when his companion whispered something in a rough voice.

Perspiration beaded Tara's forehead and nape. The men *were* from Fuad. Her hands trembled and it took everything she had to stand there, upright, instead of cowering. The sight of Raif, so strong in the face of danger, gave her strength.

'You're mistaken. Ms Michaels belongs in Nahrat.'

The younger, more agitated of the men shouted back. 'You lie. She's a Dhalkuri like us. We're taking her home.'

'I am Sheikh Raif ibn Ansar of Nahrat and I do not lie.' He paused, letting that sink in. 'I tell you now, if you try to leave without my permission, you'll be cut down by my guards.' The younger man opened his mouth but Raif ignored him. 'And we *will* uncover your

identities.' His voice deepened to an impressive reso-
nance as a savage light flared in that dark stare. 'If you
harm anyone here, you have my word, it won't just be
you who pays the price. I'll invoke the old ways. Your
families will pay as well. And if you have no families,
your friends and associates. I vow it on my family honour, on the names of all my forefathers.'

Silence engulfed the huge room. It was so thick Tara
felt it press down like a huge, invisible weight.

Now the gunmen were in whispered conference.
Their plan of an easy kidnap while the Sheikh's guard
was busy on the other side of the town was in disarray.

Tara kept her eyes on the younger one, watching
the restless jig of his fingers on the gun. Her stomach
clutched in fear.

'Your Majesty.' The older man spoke. 'We wish no
violence. It's the woman we want. We'll leave in peace
if we have her.'

For answer Raif stepped away from the wall, pacing
closer to the men and their raised weapons.

'That I can't allow. Ms Michaels is mine.' His voice
rang out, clear and forthright. Tara felt the world swoop
and dip around her. 'And,' Raif continued, 'as all the
world knows, what I have, I hold.'

Oblivious of the muffled gasps from the audience
of women, Raif turned his head, his glittering eyes
snaring hers, sending a blast of sheet lightning shear-
ing through her insides. 'That's so, isn't it, Tara? You
belong to me.'

She knew he said this for the benefit of her would-
be abductors. Yet in that strange moment, when the
world seemed to telescope around them so there was
just her and Raif, Tara felt the truth of it. The power-

ful whump of sensation, like a blow to her chest, confirmation that, yes, she belonged to him. She was tied to this man by sexual desire and by something more profound that she had no name for. A yearning that had settled deep in her bones.

'Yes,' she croaked, barely above a whisper. She lifted her chin and stepped towards him on wobbly legs. 'Yes,' she spoke louder, 'I belong to you, Raif.'

Maybe it was the use of his name, as if she really *were* his woman, but she saw the intruders' expressions alter.

'That's far enough.' The younger one waved his gun and she stumbled to a stop.

But now Raif was walking towards her, shoulders back and gait steady, as if he strolled in some grand, royal procession.

'I said—'

The older gunman stopped him, whispering urgently in his ear, his hand pushing the barrel of the gun down.

Tara felt light-headed as Raif reached her, his hand comfortingly warm as it enveloped hers. She looked up at him, torn between fear and relief, but he wasn't looking at her. His attention was fixed on the two men.

'You have my word that if you lay down your weapons and leave with me now, you will be treated humanely. You will be taken to the capital and held there while we negotiate with the Dhalkuri authorities. I will allow you to stand trial there, rather than here in my realm.'

It was an enormous concession. Especially since it was clear that these men acted under Fuad's orders. Once in Dhalkur they wouldn't be put on trial. Though

facing Fuad in a temper if they failed would make anyone tremble.

Their whispered discussion took for ever. Even with
Raif's hand holding hers, she couldn't feel calm. When
Raif squeezed her hand then released it, she almost
grabbed at him, but he approached the gunmen.

Her heart leapt in her throat, but there was a
change in their demeanour. Even the jittery younger
man looked less belligerent. Was it possible Raif's
words might persuade them? Or would they take their
chances, using her or Raif as shields? That must be
tempting, yet she'd seen the impact of his promise of
vengeance. The Sheikh of Nahrat would make an implacable enemy.

Raif spoke to them again, so low she couldn't hear.

Then suddenly, things changed. Before her widen-
ing eyes she saw the men put their weapons down and
step to one side, hands in the air. At a command from
Raif the covering over the door where he'd entered
lifted and several armed guards arrived, surrounding
the intruders.

After that everything happened quickly. The weapons and the men disappeared. Women surrounded her,
offering reassurance and undoing her bound wrists.
From them she gathered that the discreet entrance Raif
had used led to a small back room. One of the younger
women had retreated there to feed her baby before the
attackers arrived. She'd raised the alarm with Raif's
men.

It all felt unreal, even the relieved chatter of the
women and the offer of sweet tea, until she caught
sight of Raif over their heads. He was talking to a security staffer but his eyes were on her. Once more that

black stare was unreadable but Tara didn't care. She was grateful they were both unharmed. That moment when he'd walked right up to the gunmen… She'd have nightmares about that for the rest of her life.

The crowd parted and there he was. Raif, his features more drawn than usual, but reassuringly strong and solid. A great shudder racked her and she knew it was true. They really were safe.

He put his hand out and she placed hers in it, curling her fingers around his, drawing on his strength.

Raif led her out and she went with him, willingly.

CHAPTER NINE

Raif didn't draw a full breath till he had Tara back at the oasis. Her attackers were under armed escort, heading for the capital.

Used to taking charge, being the one people looked to in a crisis, he'd projected an aura of calm when dealing with the gunmen and townspeople. Yet inside he was a mess. Seeing those men threatening the defenceless women, threatening Tara…

He never wanted to face anything like it again.

Despite his show of arrogant certainty, he'd been worried his intervention wouldn't end the potentially deadly hostage drama. But he'd had to try. His gut clenched as he imagined the bloodshed if they'd tried to force their way out.

The drive to camp was silent and, though Tara hadn't dissolved into tears, her silence worried him. The sooner he got her back to the palace the better.

'We'll have you back in the city soon,' he said as they reached their tents. 'I've ordered a helicopter. We'll be back at the palace before sunset.' His own chopper had been diverted to bring in a medical emergency from an outlying area to the city and other nearby helicopters were either in use or undergoing repairs. Raif firmed his mouth. Waiting was tough but medical emergencies took priority, even now.

'I don't need to go to the city.'

Raif surveyed her pale features. 'You'll feel better somewhere safe, away from a reminder of what happened today.'

Her eyes grew huge in her face and he cursed himself for scaring her. 'You mean there's still danger?'

'No. Everything's fine.' He resisted the urge to take her hand again. Unaccountably he'd felt better with it firmly clasped in his. 'Forces have been deployed on the border and elsewhere through the province. But initial enquiries make it seem certain those two acted alone. There's no sign of anyone else.'

Raif paused, listening to the chatter of a tiny bird in the trees, feeling a tiny breeze ruffle his clothes. It was peaceful here and he knew specialists were already busy, searching out every detail on the two prisoners and how they had crossed the border.

'I'm sorry, Tara. I never guessed Fuad would make such a drastic attempt. I shouldn't have brought you.' Bile rose as he thought of how close she'd come to being taken.

'Don't apologise. You're the man that saved me, remember? Besides, you couldn't have known Fuad would try anything like this, an attempt under your very nose and in your own territory! It's outrageous. Almost…unhinged.'

Raif read the fear and outrage in Tara's face and the stew of fury in his belly stirred hotter. He'd known Fuad was ruthless, but this showed him to be obsessive, willing to risk an international incident.

'Presumably he thought a couple of men might succeed where a larger force couldn't.'

Her lovely mouth tilted up in a crooked smile that carved a hollow in his belly. 'He reckoned without considering you. I've never seen anything so brave. Thank you, Raif. I can't begin to thank you enough.'

Horrified, he raised his hand to stop her words. His bravery, if that was what it was, had been born of desperation and guilt. He'd put Tara and his people in danger. He couldn't rid himself of the horror of the moment when he'd realised the peril.

'It's over now. That's what matters.' He nodded to the tent. 'There's time for a shower before the chopper arrives.'

Tara shook her head, shafts of filtered sunlight playing on the rich mahogany tint of her hair. 'Please don't send me back. I'd like to stay.'

It was the last thing Raif expected. 'Surely you'd feel better away from what happened—'

'I don't think so. You're staying here, aren't you?'

For a second Raif thought she implied she'd rather stay where he was, then he realised Tara needed reassurance on the journey.

'I'll accompany you to the palace and see you settled.' His staff could do that but Raif remembered how she'd clung to him earlier, only releasing his hand so he could drive her here. It was nothing personal. 'Later I'll return. My business isn't finished and I want to go back tomorrow to see the townspeople are all right after today's scare.'

Tara nodded. 'I do too. They were very kind, very supportive. I'd like to visit them again and thank them.'

Raif frowned, folding his arms across his chest. He

knew she was brave. The way she'd stood alone, apparently composed, when facing her would-be abductors, proved that. But he'd felt her hand shake, seen the trembling breaths she took afterwards. Beneath her apparent calm lay distress.

'It's a nice idea. I'll pass on your thanks and good wishes. But I think—'

Once again she interrupted. She was the only person, apart from his aunt, who did that. It was still so unexpected it stopped him mid-sentence.

'Can't I think for myself? I *want* to stay.' Her eyes blazed. '*Please*, Raif. I promise to stay in the background, not make a nuisance of myself. But we left so quickly I feel bad about not staying to thank them.' Her gaze dropped. 'And even though your palace is nice, it sometimes feels like a gilded cage. I'd much rather be out here, where I can breathe.'

Stunned, he stared at this remarkable woman.

Had anyone else ever dismissed the royal palace as *nice*, preferring to stay in the desert?

Actually, now he thought about it, his mother had loved coming here with his father. She always returned to the palace with a glow in her cheeks and warmth in her eyes.

'Where you can breathe?'

She looked up. Those green eyes seemed darker, maybe because her face was pale. 'I live in London now but I spent years in small settlements, often in remote areas, wherever my father's mining work took us. I like the quiet out here and the beauty of it.' She paused. 'Besides, going back now I'd feel like Fuad was controlling me again, forcing me to cower in hiding, rather than do what I think right. Like visit those women who stood by me today.'

Raif exhaled slowly, trying to recall if anyone had so continually defied his expectations and disrupted the smooth running of his arrangements. Not that he blamed Tara for today's attack. He was the one at fault there.

She looked at him so earnestly, but he didn't miss the signs of fragility. That taut stance, as if it took extra effort to stay upright, the shadows in her eyes.

Whether she admitted it or not, Tara needed time to recover. She shouldn't be standing out here, she should be resting.

'Very well.' At his words her high shoulders dropped and a glimmer of a smile curved her lips.

'Thank you, Raif.'

His forehead crinkled and his hands curled tight as he fought the dart of pleasure he felt, hearing his name in that husky, grateful voice.

'On condition that you rest. And that, if you feel worse, you let me know.' The camp medic had checked her out but Raif was determined to look after Tara better than he had before.

'I'll be good, I promise.' Another ghost of a smile. This time he caught a hint of mischievous laughter in her expression.

An inner voice told him he wasn't interested in Tara being good. He'd much prefer her to be bad. With him.

He strode forward and yanked open the entrance to her accommodation, gesturing for her to go in. The sooner she was out of sight the sooner he might get hold of himself. Tara tempted him to forget honourable intentions.

When she was inside and only a trace of her rose and cinnamon scent lingered to tease him, Raif spoke. 'Rest now. Tomorrow we'll visit the town together. And Tara?'

'Yes?' Her voice sounded eager, despite her obvious weariness.

'For the record, you're not a nuisance.'

Once he might have thought so. Especially as she stood up to him and provoked him as no one else dared.

Now he found her perplexing, challenging, admirable, and distracting.

And dangerously tempting.

The oasis was a calm paradise. Tara heard the gentle burble of spring water as she stood in the doorway of her tent, watching diamond-bright stars pinprick the black velvet night.

The day's warm zephyr had given way to a cooler breeze that brought the indefinable scent of the desert. It teased the filmy silk caftan she'd put on after her shower, reminding Tara that beneath the crimson material she was naked.

It hadn't seemed worth dressing properly after she'd showered and washed her hair. Instead she'd curled up on the wide bed and fallen almost instantly asleep.

She'd slept through the arrival of dinner, an array of delicious dishes left on a tray.

Now, replete after grazing on the delicacies, she felt restless.

Her afternoon sleep had been plagued by disturbing dreams yet she'd woken feeling better. The light-headed, nauseous feeling of shock was gone.

Tara looked at the towering cliff beyond the oasis

and felt no fear. There'd be no more armed men coming after her. Raif would see to that.

It surprised her how implicitly she trusted him, given the doubts she'd once had. Time and again he'd proved himself an ally. Standing up for her with the Dhalkuri ambassador. Taking her under his wing and organising work in the treasury that would challenge and fascinate her.

Facing down two armed gunmen to save her.

She swallowed, her hand clutching the delicate fabric at her chest.

When she'd seen him threatening those men with vengeance, when he'd paced towards her, full of autocratic certainty, her heart had been in her mouth.

If he'd been shot because of her...

It didn't bear thinking about. Yet she couldn't banish it from her mind.

Raif was so vibrantly alive, so charismatic, it physically hurt to imagine him slumped and bloody on the floor. Which could have happened if he hadn't cowed her abductors with the sheer force of his willpower.

He was a remarkable man.

She'd never met anyone like him.

Tara *trusted* him. The knowledge filled her like bright sunlight after a long winter.

That had to be why she reacted so strongly to him. From the first he'd been larger than life. Now it felt like he'd taken over her mind. She couldn't stop thinking about him.

It wasn't just her mind he'd taken over. Her body was affected too. That was the real reason for tonight's restlessness. Today's incident had played a part, sharpening her awareness of her feelings. Of the fragility of life and how easily it could be snuffed away. She'd lost both her parents far too young. Thinking of Raif facing down those men reminded her how easily things could have ended badly.

She shivered and wrapped her arms around herself.

Today had changed things irrevocably.

Tara had been determined to keep a safe distance from Raif. Her past and her current situation making her wary. But now everything seemed stripped back, revealing the truth she'd tried to avoid.

She wanted more from Raif than protection.

She wanted far too much.

Tara was a pragmatist. She knew she couldn't have Raif's friendship permanently, much less a special place in his regard. Once she left he'd move on with his life, as she must. But she was woman enough to understand that he felt *something* for her. Something that had prompted him to kiss her. Sometimes she caught his eyes on her and read hunger there, before he saw her watching.

Desire. *That was* what made her edgy now. Suspecting Raif wanted her, even if he didn't want to want her.

Her yearning, after today's tumultuous events, felt impossible to resist. Was that what this restlessness was? A primitive acceptance that life could be short and opportunities needed to be seized?

It eclipsed her ingrained belief that temporary relationships weren't for her. That if ever she were to be with a man it would be in a loving relationship such as her parents had shared.

Tara drew a slow breath and dropped her hands, smoothing damp palms over her hips and thighs, feeling the caress of gossamer silk against bare flesh.

Instead of regaining control of her racing thoughts, the gesture made her wonder how it would feel if Raif ran his hands over her, dragging the silk against her skin. Would those powerful hands be tender or urgent?

Her nipples budded and her breasts tingled, weighted with a heaviness directly linked to the aching hollow sensation low in her body.

For so long she'd felt at the mercy of others, of circumstances she couldn't control. That was about to change.

Raif slung his damp towel over his shoulder and tugged on cotton trousers, casually tying the drawstring.

It had been a productive couple of hours.

The Dhalkuris were in prison and, in hopes of an early release, had given their names and details of how they'd crossed the border. Predictably, they hadn't admitted they were under instructions from Prince Fuad. They'd confirmed that only the two of them had entered his kingdom, yet Raif's forces were monitoring the border so closely not even a stray lamb could get through.

His mouth tightened. What the pair didn't realise was that it would be a long time before they'd be released into Dhalkur. He had no intention of letting violent offenders loose. He wouldn't send them to Dhalkur while Fuad held the reins of power.

The pair would remain imprisoned in Nahrat until Raif saw fit to release them for trial.

Preferably when Salim, rather than Fuad, took the throne.

Raif would do everything he could to ensure that happened. It was good to practise non-interference in a neighbouring state. But it was another matter when the leader of that state threatened the peace. If Fuad was made Sheikh it would be like living next door to a rabid wolf.

Raif had already contacted Salim with news from his homeland, and about Fuad's treatment of Tara. As expected, Salim had been shocked. Fuad had withheld news that their father was fading fast, obviously hoping to keep Salim out of the country so he could be crowned Sheikh unopposed. This afternoon Raif had also informed Salim of the attempted armed kidnap.

Matters were about to come to a head. Salim planned to arrive unannounced in his homeland and was meanwhile in confidential long-distance discussions with the royal council, who feared what would happen if Fuad became Sheikh.

Raif lifted the towel to rub his damp hair and strolled back into his bedroom.

He'd finish his visit tomorrow then return to the capital. He wanted Tara somewhere safe till the ructions over the border were finished and—

'Raif.'

He looked up and slammed to a halt, his heart crashing against his ribs.

'Tara?' He swallowed. For a second he'd thought her an apparition conjured by his unruly imaginings.

She stood in shadow inside the door, wearing not her usual western clothes but a dark full-length dress, her long hair around her shoulders.

His pulse beat hard in his temples. She was covered from neck to ankle yet his obstinate brain processed the sight of her and thought of sex.

'Why are you here?' His voice grated, his throat suddenly raw. He dragged the towel from his hair, holding it at his side in one clamped fist.

'I needed…' she paused, then her chin came up '…to see you.'

She stepped out of the shadows into the lamplight and everything within him stilled.

Everything except the sharp, animal instinct that turned him taut and watchful. The instinct of a hunter surveying succulent prey. Of a male scenting his mate.

His gaze traversed her, slowly, though every detail of her appearance had been branded into his consciousness in that first instant.

Her hair was a ripple of dark silk shot with reddish highlights. Her features were composed and serious, as if she'd come to parley over some vital treaty. Yet even the slight pucker of her forehead and the challenging angle of her jaw couldn't detract from the lush invitation of her sultry mouth.

A great thump of awareness reverberated through Raif. He felt it in his chest, his groin and right down to the soles of his bare feet.

The dress skimmed her curves, clinging in all the right places. The fabric must be thin because her nipples stood out against it. As she moved closer, past a lamp set on a low table, the light shone through the fabric, outlining her body in loving detail.

Raif stared. Was it wishful thinking or was she naked beneath that red dress?

'Are you unwell?'

Tara stopped and shook her head, her long hair cascading over one shoulder. 'No, I'm fine.'

She looked better than fine.

She looked—

'Are you scared? Believe me, you're completely safe here.' He'd made sure of it. There might be no guards in sight but no one could get into the oasis without being stopped. Even the air space around the encampment was closely monitored.

Another shake of her head. Raif watched her lustrous hair shimmer in the light, slipping across one pert breast. He swallowed hard, fighting the rising tide of urgent desire.

'I'm not scared. Not any more. Not with you.'

Raif breathed out in a rush, nostrils flaring and ego swelling at her words. She felt safe with him. She trusted him.

She trusted him…

'Good. Then I'll see you in the morning.'

Instead of nodding agreement as any of his subjects would have, Tara angled her chin higher, drawing attention to the line of her slender throat. How did the woman manage to appear both vulnerable and feisty?

'No. Please.' She drew a deep breath then expelled it. 'Can't I stay?'

Raif tried to concentrate on her words but his attention fell inevitably to the sweet jiggle of her unfettered breasts beneath the blood-red dress. Heat jagged through him, soldering the soles of his feet to the floor. Which was as well because he was appallingly close to forgetting his promises to himself and yanking her into his arms.

'No, you can't. We'll talk in the morning.' To reinforce the dismissal, not least to his own wayward body, he crossed his arms over his chest. 'Go to bed, Tara. I don't want you here.'

* * *

Tara was surprised at his harsh dismissal. His words cut like a lash, abrading her sensitive flesh. She shivered, suddenly cold despite the heat in her belly, and folded her arms around her body.

Raif's attention dropped from her face to her breasts. She felt the silk pull tight there. Her nipples jutted so needily that at any other time she'd be embarrassed.

But she wasn't. Because, despite his words, she'd seen the way Raif's eyes tracked her body.

The same way she'd tracked his.

She'd stood in the shadows, her mouth turning desert dry as he walked from the bathroom wearing only a pair of lightweight trousers that sat low on his hips. Every time he moved, her heart was in her mouth, wondering if they'd slide down to reveal more of his honed body.

He was a perfect study of male musculature. Tara wished she could draw so she could capture every powerful line of that rangy frame. And that tantalising dusting of hair across his muscled chest, the faint trickle of a dark line down to the waistband of his trousers. The taut abs.

Tara inhaled quickly, yanking her gaze up to his face, to discover Raif's attention straying over her body.

She'd never welcomed such frank masculine appraisal. But this was different. Tonight, it exactly matched her own needs.

'Tara, did you hear me? It's too late for talking.'

She jumped and focused her thoughts. 'I'm not here to talk.'

His eyes widened and she had the rare feeling she'd stunned him. Then they narrowed to gleaming ebony slits.

He shook his head and a muscle flicked in his jaw. 'Go, Tara. *Now.*'

Did she imagine a hint of desperation in that hard voice? Of course she did. Raif didn't do desperate.

Yet she'd come this far and she refused to retreat with her tail between her legs. Especially when she'd *seen* the interest in his glittering eyes. Felt it now in the thick atmosphere that despite the desert chill seemed to radiate heat.

Letting her arms drop, she walked up to him, so close she saw tiny beads of moisture clinging to his hair.

Tara put her hands on his shoulders and stretched up on tiptoe, her silk-clad body colliding with his hot, hard frame.

Still he didn't move, just stared down with unreadable eyes.

Nervous, she licked her lips and, remarkably, felt his powerful frame jerk beneath her touch.

'I want to stay. With you.'

Then, fearing rejection but too desperate to let that stop her, she wrapped one hand around the back of his skull. She splayed her fingers in slick, damp hair and pulled his head down to hers.

CHAPTER TEN

TARA'S LIPS TOUCHED Raif's and electricity fizzed through her, as if she'd tapped into a current. Her mouth moved against his, relearning its shape. Still he didn't move. That hard, half-naked body was unyielding, unbending.

Was he going to reject her, as he'd done after their kiss in the palace?

Had she got it wrong, imagining desire in his eyes?

Disappointment vied with desperation. She'd be utterly humiliated if he pushed her away and said he wasn't interested.

Leaning in, she slid her other hand up to his neck, mapping searing hot flesh with her palm.

Her breasts swayed against his torso, only a layer of silk separating them. It felt like the most wondrous, momentous thing in the world.

A low burr of sound teased her. Something rough and raw that she couldn't identify, till she realised she felt as well as heard it. It was a deep growl from the back of Raif's throat, vibrating into her mouth as his lips opened.

One moment he was as still as a living statue and the next he came alive in a surge of power. One arm lashed her waist, pulling her hard against him. His other hand forked through her hair, pushing it back, cupping her jaw as he tilted his head and took her mouth with ruthless efficiency.

Tara's knees gave way. She clung as he took her weight, lifting her against him. She had a second to thrill at his sheer strength, lifting her with one arm, till her thoughts frayed.

Everything was heat and ardour, the lush softness of lips, the hard thrust and swirl of tongues, the possessive grasp of Raif's hands that made her feel both aroused and secure.

Tara's fingers curled into his hair, clutching as she kissed him back.

She'd never known a kiss like it. Her experience was limited and the one time they'd kissed previously it had been…perfect.

This wasn't perfect.

It was too powerful, too utterly overwhelming for *perfect*.

This was a maelstrom she wasn't sure she'd survive.

She didn't want to survive it.

Tara wanted to lose herself in this rush of desire. A whirling kaleidoscope of sensations and desperate longing.

She inhaled sandalwood and something else rich and spicy and utterly compelling. The aroma of Raif's skin and wet hair. She felt the scorching touch of his skin. Tiny detonations of exquisite awareness peppered her flesh.

He bowed her back and she opened to him, giving everything he demanded, feeling his body press intimately against her. Between her legs bloomed moisture and that needy ache.

Tara dragged a hand down to his jaw and shivered as his skin there, textured rather than smooth, tickled her palm.

The shiver grew into a shudder as Raif broke their kiss, turning his head to plant a kiss on the centre of her palm. A deep, drawing kiss that sent more of those electric currents sparking through her.

She heaved in a gasping breath, then another, her breasts rising against his muscled chest, the glorious friction overloading her senses.

Tara's eyes snapped open and there were Raif's, black as sin and wickedly inviting, snaring hers.

She looked into that midnight gaze and wanted everything it promised. Every decadent pleasure from slow seduction to urgent ecstasy.

His mouth moved against her palm, tickling, and when he lifted his head he was smiling. Not the coolly superior half-smile he'd turned on her when she annoyed him, or the wide grin she'd seen once or twice when he was genuinely amused. This was intimate, a mere quirk at the corners of his mouth that spoke of satisfaction, or perhaps expectation. His eyes were heavy-lidded, his lips dark from their passion.

'You have three seconds to tell me you've had second thoughts.' His voice ground low, so she felt it deep in her abdomen. Even that warning felt like a caress. Because she wanted this, wanted Raif.

'I don't need three. I'm sure. I want you, Raif.'

Hyper-aware of every moment, every breath, Tara cupped his face, sliding her thumbs over the soft cushion of his bottom lip. She quivered as fire shot to her breasts and from there straight to her sex. At the feel of Raif's mouth against her skin, the realisation that he was about to give her access to his beautiful body.

His smile turned lop-sided in an expression that made her heart jangle.

'In that case, princess, your wish is my command.'

He slipped an arm beneath her legs, lifting her high against his chest. From this angle she had a scrumptious view of his decisive jaw and the chiselled planes of his face as he crossed the room.

Tara leant her head against his collarbone, wondering again how it was that with this man she didn't mind being held in a way that reinforced the disparity between them. His size and power compared with her softening eagerness.

Yet she didn't feel weak in Raif's arms. She felt triumphant, eager, and incredibly aware of her femininity.

He bent, lowering her to stand beside the bed. As he straightened, he grasped the shimmery ruby silk and drew it up her body, higher and higher. Its softness teased her sensitive flesh till he reached her shoulders and Tara obligingly raised her arms, feeling silk skim up and away.

There was an arc of colour as Raif tossed the garment away, leaving her utterly naked before him.

Tara swallowed, torn between nerves and pride. She wanted him. She wasn't ashamed of that. Yet she'd never been naked before a man.

She'd never, to her dying day, forget Raif's expression as he surveyed her.

His skin drew so taut across his features his cheekbones looked razor sharp. His nostrils flared wide and his broad chest rose hugely as he dragged in air. As if for a moment he'd forgotten to breathe and needed extra oxygen. His eyes, gleaming before, burned with a searing heat that kindled fire across her skin.

Slowly he shook his head.

Pain thudded through her chest. Was it rejection after all?

He looked so grim. So tense.

'What is it?' she whispered.

Once more Raif's mouth rucked up at one corner and her heart lurched. 'I don't have the words.' Suddenly she realised it wasn't reluctance she saw in his face but admiration. 'You're exquisite, Tara.'

The fire was inside her now, roaring along her veins. She stood straighter, chin up and shoulders back, her breasts thrusting towards him.

His hungry stare settled on her breasts and instantly that prickling, heavy sensation was back. She shifted her weight, conscious now of the plush silk carpet beneath her feet, the whispery touch of cool air on her flesh and the tiny distance between them.

'So are you.' Looking at him made her salivate. She wanted to drag her hands down his chest, feel the ridges of muscle and the soft dusting of body hair. Her fascinated gaze strayed to his pale cotton trousers, tented with his arousal.

Tara's breath hitched and held and she wondered if her lungs had forgotten how to work.

But she waited, taking her lead from him. She'd made the first move but as for the rest...

Instinct was fine but she didn't want to admit her inexperience. She had no idea how Raif would react but she wanted nothing to interrupt this. Besides, her virginity was her business.

He lifted his hand and she anticipated the touch of

long fingers on her bare breast. Instead, to her surprise, he snagged her hair, pushing it back over her shoulders, then cupped her cheek.

His expression and the gentle caress of his roughened hand against her face undid her. She swayed forward and suddenly he was there, drawing her to him.

She almost cried out at the sensation of his hot, satiny flesh against hers. The tickle of his chest hair, the delicious friction. It was too much yet not enough.

Thankfully Raif must have felt the same because a moment later they were lying on the bed, and for the first time in her life she felt a man's weight on her. Tara shuffled her legs wider and with a grunt of satisfaction he sank harder against her.

This time his kiss, while just as ardent, was slow, as if they had all the time in the world.

Tara revelled in it. She adored the taste of him. The weight of him pressing her onto the soft coverlet. The feel of him everywhere. There were so many sensations her brain was in danger of overloading.

Yet above it all, or perhaps beneath it, as it seemed to underscore everything, was the feeling Raif cherished her. He demanded but he coaxed too.

As if she needed coaxing. What she needed—

He must have had the same thought, for he lifted himself a little, propping himself up on one arm, pulling half off her to rest on his hip. Tara wanted to object. She missed the delicious sensation of his body against hers. But before she voiced a protest, his index finger tracked down to her chest, tracing around her breast in ever-diminishing circles.

Tara's breath backed up in her lungs as he leaned

down. Raif's hair was ebony in contrast to her paler skin as he put his mouth to her nipple and sucked.

She gasped, a raw sound that might have been his name, and gathered him close. She felt the flick of his tongue and that was wonderful too.

Tara squirmed, half turning on her side, trying to bring herself up against him, till he pushed his knee across her, holding her against the bed with one powerful thigh.

Her eyes widened, astonished that his superior strength, as well as his caressing mouth, should be so exactly what she wanted.

She didn't feel threatened, just aware of his power, and shockingly turned on by it.

Raif lifted his head, surveying her, and she was stunned that the sight of his lips, wet from sucking at her breast, shot a surge of wanton hunger through her.

'I want you, Raif.' Strange how the words emerged clear and even. As if she weren't teetering on the brink of something cataclysmic. She felt it in the shuddering waves coursing through her, heading down to centre on her sex.

'And you'll have me, *habibti*. Soon.'

He lowered his head to her other breast and Tara arched off the bed, as high as his restraining thigh allowed. But even that was a caress, a teasing reminder of how it would feel when finally he lay over her again and joined them.

Impatience soared. She didn't want to stop the marvellous feelings he created but she wanted…

Her mind blanked as his palm slid down her abdomen, straight through the silky hair at the juncture of her thighs, and unerringly through moist folds to that tiny, sensitive bud.

Her breath clotted as she jerked beneath him, eyes snapping wide and focusing on a lamp of filigreed metal that hung from a rafter.

Raif circled her nipple with his tongue while his finger circled her core. Every muscle and tendon in her body tightened.

Tara dragged her gaze down to find him watching her. That black gaze was a caress too, hot and sure. His lips closed on her again as he stroked her hard between her legs and suddenly, like the onset of a sudden summer thunderstorm, there was the electricity. Inside her. A current that jumped and sparked and sent her up in flames.

Her eyes closed as ecstasy took her, flinging her into another dimension where only Raif's anchoring body kept her safe.

She shuddered and cried out and through the exquisite bliss could still see Raif's glowing eyes from behind her closed lids.

Rapture took a long while to fade but eventually Tara felt herself float back to the real world. To the realisation Raif was no longer there.

Panic eased when she saw he'd moved to one side and was rolling on a condom.

The sight was fascinating. And daunting.

She tried to distract herself by pondering the fact he'd had the foresight to bring condoms. Had he expected this? Or did he take them wherever he went?

Somehow that didn't fit with what she knew of him. Raif was incredibly virile and attractive but he struck her as very selective when it came to sex.

Maybe that was her ego talking.

He saw her watching and his mouth hooked up in recognition and promise. When he moved, the weight of his lower body settled between her legs while he propped himself up on his elbows above her.

Despite the climax he'd given her, or because of it, Tara felt overloaded with sensation, absorbing the differences between them as well as the astonishing way they fitted together.

Almost fitted together. Her breath came in agitated puffs as she thought of what was to come. She wanted Raif, more than she'd ever wanted anything, yet this was uncharted territory.

His forehead crinkled. 'Okay, *habibti*?'

'More than okay,' she found herself replying. 'I was taking a moment. You feel...*we* feel...'

'Fantastic together.' His smile widened, making her insides dance and the tension disintegrate. 'But nowhere near as good as we're going to feel.' He breathed deep. Tara registered his shuddery breath and the fast tic of his pulse at his throat. 'I'm afraid it's beyond me to wait any longer.'

Something swelled high in her chest, tenderness and something much stronger. He'd given her pleasure before taking his own. His gallantry vanquished hesitation. She smoothed her palms up his bulging biceps to latch on to his shoulders.

'I don't want to wait.'

Raif took her at her word. He slipped one hand beneath her, tilting her pelvis up, and suddenly there he was, sinking into her, all that heat and power sliding flesh into flesh.

Until it felt as if something caught. Tara's lip

snagged between her teeth, her lungs stopping. Raif paused and beneath her hands his muscles turned steel-hard. She blinked and met his questioning gaze.

He was going to withdraw, wasn't he? Withdraw and send her away?

Tara's fingernails dug into his shoulders. She planted the soles of her feet on the bed and pushed up, increasing the pressure where they joined. A brief burn of pain sheared through her then Raif slipped deeper, so deep it seemed he lodged right up against her heart.

She blinked, trying to find her equilibrium, but her lungs wouldn't fill and her breath came in short gasps.

Raif slid an arm around her waist and rolled so they lay on their sides, still joined, but minus that feeling she was being crushed.

Tara drew air into starved lungs, surprised to discover that feeling of fullness, while still strange, was intriguing rather than nerve-racking.

Warm fingers brushed her cheek, pushing her long hair off her face. 'You're full of surprises, aren't you, Tara?'

Raif's ebony eyes locked on hers, unreadable but for that shimmer of heat.

'It doesn't matter.'

Part of her couldn't quite believe they were talking when their bodies—

'It *does* matter.' His voice was pure gravel. 'But not enough to stop this.' He pulled her knee higher up his thigh, then his hand found her breast as he moved against her. Tara gasped as delight coursed through her.

Raif did it again, with a slow deliberation that seemed to spin out the remarkable sensations till there was room for nothing else in Tara's brain but the wonder of it.

Again and again he pushed and now she moved her hips, anticipating each sure thrust, squirming a little at the teasing skirl of delight when he touched her...there.

'Raif?' She pulled him towards her, needing to feel him against her as little shivers set up inside.

She only had to ask once. A moment later she was on her back, Raif's body covering her like a warm blanket.

He held himself still, though the hammer beat of his heart against her chest revealed how much that cost him.

Tara lifted her head and brushed her lips against his jaw and Raif moved. His lips found hers, his kiss slow and lush as he resumed that wonderful rhythm. Shimmers of heat spread as Raif brought her closer and closer to—

The world shattered. Tara clung on tight and gasped out her pleasure. She had no words to describe the ecstasy Raif brought her, or the rolling wave of rapture that enveloped her. It was impossibly perfect.

Until Raif shuddered hard, his body pumping against her, head thrown back and superb torso strung taut. Then perfect got even better.

Still shuddering with delight, she wrapped her arms around him and hugged hard, overwhelmed by the need to assure him she was here, anchoring him. Protecting him.

It seemed the most natural thing in the world, holding Raif as she sank into the dark velvet folds of oblivion.

Raif crossed his arms and stared into the starlit night, cool air chilling his naked body. He welcomed that, welcomed anything to drag him out of the sensual fog he'd been in since Tara sauntered into his tent.

All this time he'd fought to hold back, to resist the temptation of her. Especially because of the worrying suspicion that he had begun to feel too much for Tara. More than simple desire.

Then she'd rocked up at his bedside, watched him with those sultry green eyes and said she wanted him. He had no resistance against her air of fragility mixed with feistiness.

Of course he hadn't resisted. She was a grown woman, even if his conscience whispered she was vulnerable, on the run from her cousin, traumatised by today's events.

He hitched an uneven breath as heat washed through him. Not the heat of passion but shame.

For all those reasons he should have held back.

If they weren't enough, she'd been a virgin. There'd been a moment as he entered her slick, fragrant body, when he'd met resistance and thought of pulling back. Only for a second. Because virgin or no, Raif had had to have her.

This need had simmered in his blood so long. Today's drama had only notched the heat to boiling point.

But once was definitely not enough. He wanted Tara in ways that made every other lover blur into nothingness.

He raked a hand through his hair, considering a midnight dip in the oasis's tiny pool. But it would take water frigid from an ice floe to douse his hunger for Tara.

His jaw tightened. He wasn't used to doubting his actions or second-guessing whether he'd done right.

Every cell in his body screamed that sex with Tara was the best thing he'd done in years. His thinking brain, what was left of it, knew he'd complicated everything. One way or another there'd be a price to pay.

Yet instinct told him having Tara had been inevitable from the moment she rolled out of a carpet at his feet.

With a sigh, he turned and lifted the flap of his tent. He should be thinking of how to minimise the repercussions. Instead his thoughts centred on the sight of Tara in his bed, her hair a lustrous curtain splayed across pale gold skin.

Raif's heartbeat quickened as his gaze snagged on luscious breasts, then trailed down to the indentation of her navel then further, to the hint of a dark V beneath the fine sheet.

She shifted. Jade-green eyes met his and he swore he almost heard the sizzle as his libido caught fire again.

'You're awake.' His husky voice betrayed him.

He'd thought she was out for the count.

'Yes. I went to the bathroom and had a wash.' Was that a dusting of pink on her cheeks? Did she regret what they'd done?

'Are you sore?' He swallowed, his throat scratchy.

She shook her head and that mahogany-tinted hair slid around her breasts. That, and her secretive stare from under long, dark lashes, made him harden.

Tara's gaze dropped to his groin and he swelled more.

'No, I'm not sore at all. I feel wonderful.'

Beneath the sheet she moved restlessly. Raif read the quickened rise and fall of her breasts and the way her lips parted. His own blood pumped harder, faster and in one direction.

'Excellent.'

He was at the bedside in moments. His doubts didn't stand a chance in the face of Tara, naked and inviting in his bed. He didn't give a damn about complications, political or otherwise. All he cared about was this.

Raif prowled up the bed to kneel above her. He made himself pause, waiting for assent, finding it in her smile. He leaned down and kissed her. She opened instantly, eager but in no way submissive.

Then he felt soft fingers close around him, making him judder and catch his breath as lightning shot through him.

Raif's hand clasped hers and for a moment he was tempted to teach her how to touch him there. Except he was determined that this time he'd make the pleasure last longer than a couple of minutes. For both of them.

Tugging at her wrist, he anchored it to the bed. With his other hand he stripped the sheet away then captured her other hand. She was panting now, her breasts jiggling, tempting him.

Despite his earlier performance, Raif, generally, had formidable self-control. He didn't let himself get distracted. Still shackling her hands at her sides, he moved down, kneeing her thighs open, inhaling the sweet, spicy musk scent of Tara's arousal. He tasted her, delicately at first, and even that had her writhing beneath him.

He looked up, across an expanse of golden skin, to meet wide eyes that seemed to eat him up. He licked and she jumped, a soft keening sound emerging from that sexy mouth. He licked again, wondering how it would feel if she was to return the favour, using that sultry mouth on him.

He almost came on the thought, urged on by another of her desperate cries.

Raif couldn't recall any lover testing his control as Tara did. It wasn't because of her innocence. If anything, that was a weight on his conscience. Maybe it was her enthusiasm. Yet he'd had adventurous lovers before.

Was it because she was forbidden fruit? Messing with a Dhalkuri princess was fraught with problems.

Raif gave up wondering, concentrating instead on the unique taste of her, the sound of her approaching ecstasy and the feel of her quivering body beneath him.

He'd barely started when she came apart and once more Raif had to concentrate on controlling his body's response. He waited till well after Tara had subsided into satiety before rolling over to find a condom. Condoms he'd packed because, though he'd warned himself not to pursue her, he kept imagining Tara in his bed.

He'd never imagined she'd invite herself there.

His smile was taut, almost painful, as he settled over her.

Instantly she wrapped her arms around him, her sleepy smile pure welcome.

Raif positioned himself, then, watching Tara's face, slowly drove forward, revelling in her tight heat. A ripple of muscle contracted around him. A legacy of the orgasm she'd just had?

Her smile grew and he realised she'd done it deliberately. He retaliated by covering her breast with one hand and gently squeezing. Her smile faltered.

Raif lowered his head to her mouth. Tara offered her

lips in a slow, luxurious kiss that made him forget he was the experienced one and she the learner.

They were equals in this. Equals as never before in his experience.

His brow twitched in confusion but already his body was driven by desire, not logic. He drew back then thrust again into welcome warmth, feeling her rise to meet him, circling her hips in a little shimmy that threatened to blow the back off his skull.

Where had she learned that?

The thought died as they moved again and the sensations were, if possible, even more exquisite.

Raif lingered on the brink, pride dictating he prolong this. But he reckoned without the desperate, powerful rush that hit him out of nowhere. A rush of physical sensation but something more too. Something he registered in his mind as much as his body.

A sense of relief, of excitement, of rightness.

A sense so powerful that for a second it almost eclipsed the physical pleasures bombarding him.

Then, kissing Tara with something like desperation, he moved again, taking them both over the edge into a world that felt bright and new as never before.

CHAPTER ELEVEN

TARA STOOD BESIDE Raif as the town elders welcomed them, and wondered how everything could seem the same when everything had changed.

Raif still looked every inch a ruler and she...well, the mirror this morning had shown she looked the same, if you discounted a slight flush in her cheeks, and lips that looked a little fuller.

In one night she'd become addicted to the taste of Raif. And to other things: the hard press of his athletic body, the magic of them moving together, and the husky sound of his voice in her ear as he caressed her and made her boneless first with longing, then with satisfaction.

Nor was the change just about physical awareness. There was something more. Something profound that she had no name for and didn't want to think about. When she thought of Raif, which was all the time, she felt...

No, this wasn't the time to examine her feelings. Especially as she suspected she'd be uncomfortable with what she discovered.

She stiffened her knees, standing taller.

Instantly Raif turned his head to look at her. He'd

been like this all morning, as if their night together left him attuned to any shift in her mood. As with his touch, it made her feel precious, but it scared her that he was so hyper-alert to her emotions as she still grappled with them.

Gleaming black eyes snared hers. Tara's breath backed up into her lungs as she read concern and intimacy there. He'd looked at her that way all morning.

Raif had wanted her to stay behind, saying she'd feel better for a rest after her sleepless night.

It was true she felt a little wobbly, but not in a bad way. In a glorious way.

Did she sway? It was hot in the sun and she'd taken off her sunglasses for the official welcome. For a second the shadows seemed to stir then she felt Raif's hand at her elbow, holding her steady.

She sent him a grateful smile then froze. He shouldn't touch her, should he?

But no one seemed to notice. Maybe things were different in Nahrat. In Dhalkur no one touched the Sheikh in public and nor did he touch anyone else. Handshakes were usually limited to other heads of state.

Then she remembered the way he'd led her into the grand dining salon with his hand at her elbow. Clearly the rules were different here.

Raif squeezed her elbow and she relaxed. He thanked the town elders for their welcome and they entered the town, heading towards the square.

It looked completely different.

Yesterday the open space had obviously been swept and tidied for the royal visit. But today it was transformed.

Bright banners fluttered everywhere and all around

the square stood potted plants, some heavy with citrus fruit and others with roses. Tara guessed householders had brought in their precious, carefully tended plants. Gardens were hugely prized in this arid region and the townspeople had created an amazing, if temporary, one. There were even pots of herbs scenting the air.

A huge awning extended from the community centre out into the square and deep in its shade sat two cushioned chairs. Around it stood what looked like the whole population. Sunlight gleamed on traditional curved knives tucked into the men's belts. It sparkled off the women's jewellery. Some wore scarves sewn with gold coins and medallions. Others wore long, handsome heirloom necklaces, and in the hush Tara heard the tinkle of bracelets.

'Raif?' She kept her voice low. 'What's happening?' Yesterday people had been neatly, if soberly clothed. Today they were dressed for a festival.

He didn't turn his head and in profile his proud features looked almost stern. But then, he was facing into the sun.

'A celebration.' He paused. 'They're glad to see us after what happened yesterday.' Tara nodded, understanding the need to rejoice after coming so close to violence the day before. 'Relax and enjoy it.' Raif turned to her, his lips curving up into a disarming smile that made her wish they were back in his bed, naked.

Did he read her thoughts? Hunger flared in those midnight eyes. Her lips parted as she inhaled the spice scent of Raif's warm flesh and sandalwood soap. A shiver raked from her nape to the soles of her feet.

'Hold that thought, *habibti*.' His voice was so low she might have imagined it if she hadn't seen his lips move. 'Later.' His fingers tightened on hers, squeezing. Then he drew her forward towards the crowd.

The next hour passed in a blur. There were so many people to meet. Even strangers from outlying villages had been drawn in. And after making their obeisance to their Sheikh, it seemed they all wanted to see her too. Tara lost track of the number of people she spoke to, babies she admired and smiles she returned.

She was especially glad to see those women who'd been with her yesterday. But when she thanked them for their support, they shook their heads and said they'd done nothing. Even the women with bruised faces, who'd tried to prevent Tara's abduction, made light of their actions.

Yet Tara felt warmed by what they'd done, and the way they crowded around today, checking on her and apologising that something so terrible should happen in their town.

She had a moment of stark shock when several offered congratulations, wishing her and Raif a happy future together. Her face flamed as she explained Raif's words had been solely to free her.

The women were delighted when Raif joined her, temporarily leaving the men. He put them at ease, insisting a frail, elderly lady take a seat in the shade.

This was a different man to the one she'd seen before. He was still an authority figure, but away from the pomp of the palace, among ordinary people, Raif was relaxed and approachable.

He chatted with everyone from local officials to new mothers, from young men hoping to work in an enterprise he'd organised, to the poorest of the poor.

There was dancing and a display of marksmanship that Raif took part in. Tara wondered why she was surprised. His people liked and respected him and it seemed the feeling was mutual. Today he wore a smile more often than a frown and there was no sign of that blank, imperious stare.

Tara saw not a sovereign but a man. Watching him laugh with rival sharpshooters made her wonder how much Raif's responsibilities weighed on him. When did he get time to relax?

An image filled her head, of Raif lying spent, chest heaving, his flesh hazed with sweat, a satisfied smile curving his mouth. *Then* he'd been relaxed.

Abruptly Raif turned his head. Their eyes met.

There it was again. That whump of connection.

A moment later he was forging through the crowd towards her. 'Ready to go?' he murmured.

'Yes, please.' She looked around. 'But before we leave, I think you should explain to them. Some of the women believed what you said yesterday about me being your woman.'

'I've spoken to the elders. Don't worry. They understand the situation exactly.' Raif's eyes held hers and heat pulsed through her. 'Right now we have other priorities.'

Fire kindled at his look. Heat rose like a tide from her breasts to her cheeks.

His smile widened. Fifteen minutes later, they were on their way.

'This isn't the way to the oasis.'

Beside her at the wheel, he nodded. 'You've got a good sense of direction.'

'It's easy to tell. We're not on a paved road.' She

looked ahead where a companion vehicle rounded a curve. 'From the direction of the sun we're heading away from the oasis.'

'Not everyone would realise that.'

'I've lived in remote areas. Learning to orientate yourself is an important survival skill.'

Raif slanted her a glance. 'You seem disappointed.'

She was. The look he'd given her and his talk of other *priorities* made her assume—

A warm hand covered hers, his thumb stroking her wrist. Instantly she felt breathless and shivery.

She bit her lip, suddenly unsure about admitting her desire. Last night and this morning Raif had made intimacy easy. But despite those moments in the town when she'd felt that familiar communion with him, she'd also been reminded of the gulf between them.

'I'm disappointed too, Tara.'

'You are?' She swung around to see his eyes on her before he turned back to the road.

'I want nothing more than to be alone with you, *habibti*.' The endearment feathered through her insides like a caress. 'Today's festivities tested my patience to the limit. I'd rather have been back in our bed.'

Our bed. Crazy how his choice of words buoyed her.

Tara turned her hand and clasped his. 'Then why not go to the oasis?'

'Don't tempt me. You don't know how close I am to doing just that.' He withdrew his hand and put it on the wheel. 'We couldn't stay at the oasis indefinitely. We're returning to the capital. Apart from anything else, that means I can have you completely to myself without interruption.'

Tara shivered at the promise in his deep voice.

'Apart from anything else?'

He shrugged. 'Communications are better at the palace, if there's any more trouble from Fuad. Plus I want to speak with your cousin Salim again.'

'You've spoken with Salim?' That surprised her. 'I thought you weren't friends?'

'Acquaintances more than friends, but he needed to know how ill his father was. Fuad had kept the full gravity of the situation from him.'

Tara nodded. That was typical of Fuad. 'You're calling him now to tell him about the attempted kidnap?'

'He already knows. I sent a message yesterday. He has to know how desperate his brother is.' Raif paused for a beat. 'But it's better if I'm on hand in the capital if he needs assistance or advice.'

In other words, if Fuad tried anything desperate again. Tara shivered, rubbing her hands up her arms, feeling the tenderness where bruises still lingered.

'So you're supporting Salim? I thought you didn't want to play politics?'

Raif steered the vehicle around a tight curve as they crested a ridge. 'I don't. But I'd rather have a reasonable man running Dhalkur than someone as unstable as Fuad. Besides, I'm involved whether I like it or not.'

'I'm sorry.' Tara clasped her hands in her lap, remembering how he'd been forced to face the ambassador when she'd broadcast her presence in the palace. 'I didn't mean to embroil you in all this.'

'I know you didn't. It's okay.'

She shook her head. 'It's not. I've brought nothing but trouble.' A hard weight filled her chest as she remembered Raif facing those armed men, basically challenging them to shoot him. Tara swallowed, trying and failing to eradicate the metallic tang of fear. 'You should never have had to confront those men. What were you thinking, putting yourself in danger?' Her voice rose. 'You should have left it to the professionals.'

And let it end in a siege and bloodbath?

But he heard the tremor in her voice and knew Tara needed comfort, not an argument. He covered her hands again, noting how chilled they were. Strange that yesterday, though obviously shocked, she'd seemed to recover quickly. Was this delayed reaction?

Raif pulled over to the hard edge of the road and switched off the engine. Turning, he saw defiance and vulnerability in her tense features. Was there ever a more challenging woman?

For the last three hours he'd been torn between wanting sex and worrying over the new complication today's celebration had highlighted. Now both those faded from his mind.

'It's over, Tara. You're safe and so am I. There'll be no more incursions across the border, no one coming to snatch you. Precautions have been taken.'

Her mouth crimped in a crooked line. 'You think *that's* what worries me?'

She blinked, her eyes glittering brighter than usual. Despite what she'd been through, he'd never seen her cry. Yet she was moved by strong emotion.

Raif drew a slow breath as it struck him she was upset *about him*. He'd let her earlier words about him leaving the situation to the professionals wash over him as a platitude. It was only now, looking into accusing green eyes, that he realised the depth of her fear.

For him.

Something grabbed at his belly. A feeling he didn't recognise. Warmth suffused him, and tenderness. It seemed remarkable that, in the midst of her own troubles, Tara was concerned about him.

Because she cared.

Raif's breath expelled, only to rush back so quickly that for a second he felt dizzy.

He could count on the fingers of one hand the people who cared for him personally. Oh, there were people who'd miss him as Sheikh if he died. He was generally popular. And there were lots who saw it as their duty to look after him. But there had been no one close since his parents died. Apart from his aunt and a few good friends, no one who'd feel his loss personally.

Raif froze as he digested this strange sensation. Tara's fear for him, and his concern to minimise her distress.

His feelings were more than the usual need to do the appropriate thing. This was personal, on a level he'd never experienced.

Her hands turned beneath his, her fingers gripping so tight he knew she was reliving those moments staring down the barrel of a gun.

'Why would you *take* such a risk? You could have ended up dead in a pool of blood. Talk about reckless—'

'Shh. It's over now. Everyone is safe.' He lifted his hand to her jaw, feeling her throbbing pulse.

'But why were you so foolhardy? I couldn't believe it when you spoke to them that way.'

Raif undid his seatbelt and leaned across, brushing her mouth with his. Tara's breath was a sweet exhalation as if of relief, then her lips moved tentatively against his.

That unfamiliar feeling intensified—that grabbing at his gut, and the heat welling in his chest, the tingling in his blood.

He deepened the kiss and she met him halfway. Gone was her hesitation, replaced by the confident woman she'd been last night, inviting herself into his bed.

Except it hadn't been so simple. Tara had been a virgin and, once the first flush of arousal wore off and he'd been able to think, he'd registered her lack of experience.

How had he not seen it?

Simple. He hadn't wanted to because that would mean stopping, and he was too selfish for that.

Now he leaned in, gathering her close, deepening the kiss, revelling in the rising tide of delight that obliterated every concern as she pressed against him. Her mouth was both sweetly yielding and demanding.

Till her seatbelt obstructed him. Tara gave a muffled sound of frustration and fumbled at the clasp.

But the moment pierced his self-absorption.

Raif was used to indulging in sex without interruption. He *never* stole kisses in the middle of an official convoy where his security team would be scoping out what had made him stop his vehicle, setting up an observation post to ensure no one came near. He *never* kissed a lover in public. He was always discreet, ensuring his lovers' names didn't become fodder for gossip.

And here he was, necking on a public road.

He covered Tara's hand and reluctantly drew back.

'Best not.' He met her unfocused eyes and felt desire vie with duty. 'Not here, where anyone could see us.'

Tara turned to stare at the deserted road, deserted because his staff would have stopped any traffic. She looked dazed. Which was how he felt.

This attraction was rooted far deeper than anything in his experience. It was about feelings as much as sexual desire. Which made it unique.

Damn it. He didn't have the time for unique or for a relationship. This morning had revealed he had a PR situation of monumental proportions to manage, on top of a desperate lunatic poised to take command of the neighbouring kingdom. And still he wanted to forget common sense and sink back into Tara's lush kiss.

A chill feathered his spine. Was this how his grandfather had felt, driven by feelings for the one woman who could blind him to duty and responsibility? Who'd lured him into the illusion of love to the detriment of all else?

Raif frowned and sat back, annoyed at how tough it was to move away from Tara. In broad daylight. With his entourage waiting and guessing the cause of the delay.

This felt like loss of control. It *was* loss of control. A complete anathema to a man whose life was about leadership and duty.

He thrust aside the thought of his grandfather. Raif could handle this. He could have Tara and maintain control.

'I want you, Tara,' he ground out. 'But let's wait till we're home.'

He'd never kept a lover in his home before. Always he conducted his liaisons away from the palace. It was another difference from his previous relationships and it felt significant.

'Good thinking.' Her voice sounded shaky but he couldn't read her features as she lifted her hands to smooth her hair then, discovering the damage his questing hands had caused, taking out the pins to let it down.

Raif watched transfixed as she began plaiting those long tresses. How could the mere sight of her fixing her hair undo him? Because it reminded him of the feel of that silken hair wrapped around him in the night? How it had felt in his hands as he'd lost himself in her sweet body?

Abruptly he tugged his seatbelt and snapped it closed, then started the engine.

The four-wheel drive topped the next rise and there was the first vehicle in his entourage pulled over, waiting. It moved out onto the road and led the way. A few seconds later Raif saw in his rear-view mirror the next vehicle in the convoy.

Had they seen him kissing Tara?

He wasn't ashamed of Tara, or what they shared, yet Raif didn't like turning her into an object of speculation.

His mouth twisted in a grim smile. Too late. He'd already done that. By claiming her as his yesterday, before scores of witnesses, he'd thrown her straight into the public eye.

'Raif?'

'Yes?'

'I understand the theory of why you walked in unarmed yesterday. I know what your intentions were.'

Raif silently congratulated her. That was more than

he'd done at the time. Oh, he'd weighed the options and made a considered choice, but in reality he'd been compelled by a force stronger than logic. He'd simply known he had to save her.

'But I can't imagine how you'd think it would work, or how you could *do* that. Calmly walk in and confront those men, putting your own life on the line.'

It really was worrying Tara. Raif opened his mouth to remind her that it was over and they were safe, then reconsidered. She needed an explanation.

He didn't want to try to explain the urgent need he'd felt to protect her, no matter what the odds. Instead he stuck with the obvious.

'It's what I was trained for. I was raised to step in when necessary and not shirk my responsibilities.'

'But you're not a hostage negotiator!' There it was again, distress colouring her voice.

'Actually, I do have those skills. But my real experience is in diplomatic and trade negotiation. I negotiate all the time, when my people bring problems and expect me to solve them.'

'That doesn't explain why you'd walk, unarmed, into danger. You've got a whole team employed to protect you!'

He shot her a sideways glance. 'Leadership is a two-way street. I'm protected and enjoy the many benefits of being Sheikh, but I have to be ready to protect my people.'

Raif paused, seeking words to explain. 'My father raised me to understand that, behind the pomp and glamour, I have a duty to Nahrat. Even at a cost to myself. I must be ready to make a sacrifice if necessary.'

'I doubt many world leaders would do what you did.'

He lifted his shoulders. Few were put in such situations.

'Maybe I take my responsibilities more seriously since I inherited the throne early. I've striven to be a leader my father would have been proud of.'

Raif stopped, surprised to hear the admission. It wasn't something he'd voiced before, yet, sitting here with Tara, it seemed natural to speak of such things, to make her understand.

'You loved him,' she murmured.

'Yes. Him and my mother both.'

It had been tough losing them. He'd missed them terribly. They'd been a close-knit family and, despite his aunt's care, even she didn't fully understand the burdens of kingship.

Raif had been petrified of doing the wrong thing. He'd listened hard to his advisers and his temporary regent, training to be the best Sheikh he could be, always asking himself what his father would do in difficult situations.

'It must have been terribly hard to lose them at a young age.'

Surprising how her sympathy pierced the emotional armour he'd worn so long. For a second he felt it again, the raw grief and fear, but at the same time Tara's understanding felt like balm.

'It was a long time ago.'

'Does that matter? Losing your parents is a blow, whenever it happens.'

It was a reminder that Tara still grieved for her mother.

Guilt snaked through Raif's belly. It reminded him of the serpentine hiss of his conscience last night as

Tara slept beside him. That voice had deplored his self-ishness, taking advantage of a virgin newly alone in the world and on the run from a sadistic cousin. It taunted, saying no decent man would have behaved as he had.

Quickly, he changed the subject. 'Maybe because I acquired the habit of authority early that gives me a different perspective.'

He heard a huff of laughter. 'You can say that again. One thing I've noticed about you, Raif, is that you always expect to get your own way.'

The humorous note in Tara's voice relieved some of the tightness in his chest. 'You'd prefer a man who can't make up his mind? Or who doesn't have the strength to stand up for what he believes in? I think not.'

Tara might argue with him but those arguments held an undercurrent of sparking awareness. Tara gave as good as she got. She'd be bored with a man who gave in to her all the time.

From the corner of his eye he saw her shake her head. 'There has to be a happy medium. The way you strolled in yesterday, as if you owned the place—'

'I do. It's my country, remember? My people. I had to act. I couldn't allow Fuad's thugs to take you.'

Tara's indrawn breath hissed. 'I still don't know how to thank you properly. I can't believe what you did for me.'

Her fingers curled around his forearm and he turned to meet her serious face. She looked lost, her eyes huge.

Something shifted inside Raif. He needed to wipe that look away.

Deliberately he pinned on a knowing smile and raised her fingers to his lips. 'As for thanks, I'm sure we can arrange something in the privacy of the palace.'

Her laughter told him he'd distracted her for the moment. Yet his thoughts returned inevitably to the implications of yesterday's actions.

Tara thought him brave or foolish to walk in unarmed. Yet it had been the only way he could think of to save her. Claiming Tara as his had worked. Because her captors, like his subjects, understood what it meant when the Sheikh of Nahrat publicly claimed a woman as his.

In their eyes he wasn't talking about a mistress, but a wife.

That was what had saved her. The kidnappers had known there'd be no escape from retribution, ever, if they took Raif's spouse. That he'd pursue them mercilessly and with all the force of his authority. His forebears had a reputation for being just, but when crossed they were renowned for ferocious ruthlessness.

It was as well Tara didn't yet fully understand the reason for today's festivities. He'd let her think the townsfolk were celebrating a peaceful end to the siege and squashed her qualms that some believed she was his woman.

Because now definitely wasn't the time to tell her. She was distressed by yesterday's events, still shocked. He'd explain later, when she was less agitated and they could talk it through without possible interruption. Besides, he didn't want a scene in public.

He'd find the right time, *later*.

Everything had changed irrevocably. News of what had happened would fly faster than the wind across the desert.

Today's celebration was just the beginning.

As far as his people were concerned, he'd chosen Tara as his bride.

CHAPTER TWELVE

RAIF DIDN'T MANAGE time alone with Tara when they reached the palace. That fantasy he'd had—of taking her straight to bed—was just that, a fantasy. The sort of thing an ordinary man might do. Not the ruler of a nation.

He sighed, rolling his shoulders as he finally headed towards her suite. It had been a long afternoon.

At least he'd seen her settled before turning to the urgent matters waiting for him. It wasn't till she was safely in her rooms at the heart of the palace that Raif admitted his relief.

There'd been no danger to her today. He'd taken every precaution to ensure that. But seeing her in his home, knowing that here no one could harm her, Raif had felt some of the tension hugging his shoulders roll away.

How was it that a woman he'd known such a short time affected him so?

His usual preference was for tall blondes and, though he chose intelligent woman as his lovers, they never tested his patience as Tara did. She seemed to go out of her way to get under his skin.

Perhaps it was the combination of intriguing, attractive woman and challenge. Or the dramatic circumstances of her arrival.

Or perhaps it was something altogether different. Raif enjoyed a challenge as much as the next man but his feelings for Tara were deeper than that. As for the drama that surrounded her—he had no need for more excitement.

This was about Tara herself. She drew him. Her body, definitely. Her personality, surprisingly yes. He'd never known a taste for stubborn, feisty women, but in Tara her verve was something he relished. Her care of him...that was something new, but instead of being disturbed by it, Raif welcomed it.

He'd never known feelings like these, so he had no compass to follow. Previous experience indicated that his fascination must wear off, as he'd never had a lover he wanted permanently. On the other hand, he'd need to choose a wife some time and circumstances had forced him to choose Tara.

Circumstances?

Honesty forced him to admit he could have left the rescue to his expert team. The odds were they'd have ended the siege without injuring the hostages.

Except those odds hadn't been enough. Raif couldn't contemplate any risk to Tara.

He'd claimed her in the heat of the moment, but he'd been fully aware of what he was doing. He'd walked into the situation with his eyes wide open and didn't regret it.

Raif hadn't known her long, but he'd been with her through crises. Times of stress provided a unique opportunity to see the core of a person.

In Tara he saw a woman who was honest, who had

courage and tried to be indomitable. He admired her loyalty, the way she'd been almost more concerned for the man who'd brought her over the border than herself, fretting over whether he'd been set free. Nor was she interested in Raif's wealth. Tara might be an expert on jewellery but she'd never hinted that he might give her an expensive gift. The woman was even determined to pay him back for the clothes his staff had procured!

She was vivacious yet kind, as he'd seen in her interactions with his staff and citizens. Plus, she could hold her own at a royal event. She was a quick learner with an innate sense of self-worth that would help if he made her his Queen.

As would her royal lineage, for it was still expected that the Sheikh would marry someone from a significant family.

Raif paused a few paces from her door.

Was he really going to do it? Take Tara Michaels as his bride?

It was an unorthodox match. Some would baulk at his marrying a woman from Dhalkur. This afternoon he'd fielded concerns from a number of respected advisers. Yet for everyone who bemoaned such a royal bride there was another who applauded what they saw as an attempt to bury the enmity between the two nations.

Ultimately the decision was Raif's.

Did he want to be shackled with an obstinate, independent, foreign wife?

His preference was to have Tara as his lover. Raif hadn't planned to marry yet. But he *did* want Tara.

His chest tightened as he wondered if his feelings bore some resemblance to his grandfather's weakness.

But Raif wasn't allowing personal emotion to undermine logic. He was weighing the pros and cons.

He looked at the door to her suite, thought of her waiting for him, wearing that eager, almost flirtatious expression she'd turned on him this morning.

Raif's brain slowed as other parts of his body responded.

His options were limited. He accepted the situation or removed Tara from the palace straight away, in the process losing face with his people. As far as they were concerned, he'd promised himself to this woman.

He thought of those green eyes that gave a window into her thoughts and desires, her lush mouth, and the rush of attraction between them.

Raif's mouth curled in a slow smile.

He strode towards her suite.

Tara answered the door within moments.

Had she been waiting for him?

Her dress, the colour of dark grapes, clung to her sensational curves. Her lustrous hair spilled around her shoulders almost to her waist, making his palms tingle as he imagined sifting it through his fingers. Her eyes were veiled by long lashes but her ripe lips wore that sultry pout that turned him inside out.

'Tara.' There was a world of want in the word and he barely cared.

Her chin rose, her lashes lifting, and he read both hesitation and need in her expression.

He understood the feeling. Their situation should make him hesitate too. How much more complicated for her, who'd been a virgin last night, and was still dependent on his charity for her safety?

'I missed you.' It was remarkably easy to admit.

Instantly he was rewarded by a smile that made his chest pound and his mouth dry. Such a little thing to pack so much power.

'I missed you too.' Her voice was husky.

Raif lifted his hand to that shining hair, winding it around his fist. He tugged, gently, and she came.

This close the rapid rise and fall of her breasts was a teasing caress, making his lungs stall on a sharp inhale. The scent of roses and cinnamon, and warm, willing woman, sneaked into his nostrils, shutting down his capacity for higher thought.

'You were gone so long.' Her pout was back, igniting a sizzle that ran straight to his groin.

'I had urgent things to sort out. But I came as soon as I could. No one will interrupt us now. We have all night.'

The thought should have been an incentive for him to take his time but instead his hunger was urgent.

'I want you, Tara.' Desperately, but he managed at least to keep that word between his lips.

'Good.' Her brow puckered in a hint of a frown that he found ridiculously adorable. 'I've been waiting and waiting.' Her mouth crimped. 'I thought you might have changed your mind.' Raif had to bend his head to hear her final words.

He shook his head as he looped his free arm around her waist and held her against him. He saw the moment she felt the press of his erection and was intrigued to see colour warm her cheeks.

Tara was such a fascinating mix, of eagerness and innocence, of feistiness and compliance. If he took her as his, life wouldn't always be easy. She'd argue and expect things he mightn't want to give. She'd make up her own mind, which meant he'd have to negotiate and persuade.

But what was life without challenges?

'There was urgent business I had to see to, but believe me, *habibti*, through it all I thought of you.'

Wrapping both arms around her, he lifted her off her feet. Her eyes popped wide then she looped her arms around his neck and pressed a kiss to his jaw.

Longing shivered through him. An urgency to have this woman *now*, to claim her as his own.

He didn't make it to the bedroom. Barely made it to the first long sofa. They collapsed onto it, Raif taking her weight then rolling on the deep cushions to pin her beneath him.

The body-to-body contact shredded his control, undermining his intention to make this last. Instead he pulled back, skimming his hands down to her thighs and tugging her dress up.

His breath came out in a whoosh as the hem rose to her waist and he saw she was naked beneath it.

'You're not wearing underwear,' he croaked out.

'I was expecting you to come, so it didn't seem worth bothering.' Her mischievous tone drew his gaze to her eyes. Gone was the diffident innocent, in her place a delightful siren.

Oh, he was definitely going to come. 'Excellent. I hope this turns into a habit.'

With a shudder of terrible need, he reefed the dress up and off her body, leaving her naked and alluring. One delicate hand moved across her breasts as if she contemplated covering herself.

'Don't. Let me admire you.' Raif caught her hand and put it on his belt buckle while his eyes ate her up.

His breath disintegrated as she started unbuckling his belt then strove to undo his trousers that now stretched tight across him. Her hands brushed him and Raif discovered it was the most arousing foreplay he'd ever experienced.

With one quick movement he hauled his shirt over his head, tossing it aside. By the time he had a condom out of his pocket she'd pulled his zip down.

Rolling to one side, he sheathed himself then drew a deep breath that trembled on the brink of surrender. This would be quick, but not so quick he sacrificed Tara's pleasure for his.

He stroked between her legs, delighting in the slick dampness he discovered and the inviting way her thighs fell open. Now all he had to do was hold off long enough to—

'Don't!' Tara clutched his wrist as if to stop him, though her hips lifted off the bed towards his caress.

'What's wrong?' The words almost choked him. His blood was thickening, his brain clogging.

She tugged his hand and he let her pull it away. 'I'm so ready I can't last if you do that. I want you inside me.'

Never had Raif been so eager to oblige. He fell between her soft thighs and had to grit his teeth against the urge to spill himself there and then. Tara's knees lifted around his hips then he felt her ankles on his back as he surged forward and joined them in a single stroke that was so easy, so right, it felt profound.

'More,' she whispered against his collarbone and he gave it, withdrawing and returning, deep and slow and so satisfying that already he felt the flutter of her climax begin.

Raif told himself it was satisfaction he felt and anticipation as his body responded to the slick, tight embrace of hers. But there was much more. Tenderness and...

His thoughts frayed as she bucked up against him, precipitating an avalanche of sensation.

Instinctively he curled an arm around her, holding her to him as he took her mouth in a desperate kiss that mirrored the wild plunge of their bodies.

There was a blast of white-hot light, a mighty tremor as if the earth shook deep beneath the citadel, but Raif was barely aware of either. His only consciousness was bliss and the scents, feel, taste and sound of Tara joining him in ecstasy.

The next morning, Tara decided that if she let herself think about it, she'd worry she was addicted to this man. Even the approving way he watched her from under lazy lids as she brushed her hair made her feel different. Powerful, like some Scheherazade who so easily entranced her lover, yet at the same time incredibly self-aware, conscious that she was out of her depth with Raif.

He was a king and she a sales assistant. He was used to ordering and being obeyed and she was used to thinking for herself. He was a sensual, generous, experienced lover and she had nothing to guide her during intimacy but instinct and observation of how Raif responded to her touch.

Yet those thoughts crowded to the back of her mind when they made love, or chatted desultorily. When he spooned her body against his and fell asleep holding her.

Or when he faced down armed intruders to save her.

Something shuddered through her, the same emotion she'd been trying to ignore for days, but it wouldn't fade.

Tara yanked her mind back to the present, telling herself there was no time to dwell on that. Not with Raif here, watching her dress.

She'd never before realised that having a man watch you dress could be as arousing as having him strip your clothes away, something at which Raif was expert.

'You're beautiful, Tara.' His smile lingered, then he flicked a glance at his watch before straightening the cuff of his richly embroidered bronze silk coat, making her wonder if he was nervous.

The idea was impossible. Raif stood tall and proud in his magnificent clothes, his features relaxed, his eyes gleaming as they took her in.

She was the one who felt nervous.

'Are you going to explain what's happening?' It was mid-morning and she'd barely surfaced after an incredible night of lovemaking. Her legs felt a little wobbly and she had that floaty feeling that she'd discovered came from intimacy with Raif. He'd spent the whole night with her, sharing breakfast in her suite, then leaving her to catch up on sleep while he went off for meetings.

An hour ago, he'd returned. Twenty minutes later, in the shower, holding her against him after she sobbed out her ecstasy, he'd announced they had an appointment in another part of the palace. He'd asked her to wear something stunning, since there would be photographers.

Deciding it was tied up with proving to Fuad that

she wasn't returning to Dhalkur, Tara complied. There was something about Raif now, a tightly leashed energy, that told her this was important to him. Infuriatingly he refused to explain yet, saying he would when the moment was right. She owed him so much, it seemed paltry to cavil.

Tara found a dress of teal green that fell in soft folds to just below her knees. Tiny beads in teal, jade and a shade of rich blue adorned the bodice, catching the light when she moved.

Now, as Raif looked again at his watch, she twisted her hair high into an upswept style that she hoped looked classically elegant.

She had no jewellery but the dress was so feminine and sumptuous she didn't think it mattered.

She opened her mouth to ask if the outfit would do when he beat her to it.

'You look perfect, *habibti*. I'm honoured to accompany you.' Raif lifted her hand and bent over it, touching it with his lips and forehead in a courtly gesture that made her heart somersault.

Caution warned that she was in too deep. That she should at least set some ground rules for this affair. But she had no idea what they'd be. She loved being with Raif. Loved everything about the way he made her feel. Loved...

Tara drew in a sharp breath, stunned at the dangerous direction of her thoughts.

However wonderful this interlude, their paths lay in different directions. Raif's in Nahrat and hers... Well, she had yet to find out where she'd go. She was almost sure London wasn't for her. But she'd work it out later.

Pinning on a smile to hide the sudden dip of distress inside, as if she'd taken a step into nothingness, she turned to Raif. 'I'm ready.'

How had she ever thought his eyes cold? His expression was so warm she felt an answering flush suffuse her. It wasn't even sexual, it was…affectionate? Tara blinked, wondering if she read too much into his satisfaction.

But there was no time to probe, for he linked her arm through his and led her out of the room.

Tara was hyper-aware of Raif's tall frame next to hers, the way he shortened his stride for her. That warmth within intensified into something else. Something strong and true.

For a second Tara acknowledged the emotion, even named it. She swallowed hard as the truth of it resonated through her.

Then, with a shiver that traced from her nape to her soles in her new shoes, she blocked those thoughts.

That particular emotion, for this man, could only spell disappointment and unhappiness. She couldn't dwell on it now. It was impossible.

Later, when she had leisure to think, distress would hit, and desperation.

For now all she could do was put on a brave face and hope he wasn't perceptive enough to realise she felt far more than lust for him.

As they approached the public rooms first one then another courtier appeared in the doorways, bowing as they passed. Raif inclined his head and kept walking.

Tara looked around, puzzled. 'What's going on?' she whispered.

'They're paying their respects,' he murmured, leading her into a familiar sitting room. 'Don't worry, I'll

explain soon.' A door on the other side was open and
Tara recognised the balcony where last week she'd
leaned out, enjoying the view of the city, only to create a furore of speculation.

A figure moved towards them. It was the chamberlain, bowing deep to Raif, then, to Tara's astonish-
ment, to her.

'Everything is ready, Your Majesty.' He turned to
her and smiled. It was the first time he'd done so. 'Ma-
dame.' Then, before she could question him, he bowed
out of the room.

'Raif? What's happening? I don't understand.' Un-
ease feathered her spine.

Beside her Raif drew a deep breath. Beneath her
arm his was rock hard. With tension? 'Is everything
okay? Is there some problem? Has Fuad caused trouble for you?'

A wry smile carved deep grooves in his cheeks but
there was no humour in his eyes. They looked serious.
'I find it refreshing that your concern is for me, *habibti*,
after all you've been through.'

His expression grew tender and Tara basked in it.
Once more it felt as if her heart rolled over in her chest.
How had she come to care about him so much?

She had no idea, only knew she did.

She cared. Too much.

Tara had a terrible feeling her heart might crack
when it was time for her to leave.

He drew a slow breath and covered her arm with his
hand. 'My people want to see you. They've travelled
from outside the city to do so. I thought we'd have more
time to prepare before this happened but they're even
more eager than I anticipated.'

Tara became aware of a dull murmur from beyond the open windows. It was a low roar of sound that reminded her of the swell of the sea. Except they were inland. Her skin prickled.

'Why would they want to see me?'

For a second it seemed he wouldn't answer. A muscle flicked in his jaw and his nostrils flared as he took a deep breath. Then his dark gaze captured hers. 'Because I claimed you as my woman. By Nahrati custom that makes you my bride.'

CHAPTER THIRTEEN

'BRIDE?' TARA FELT her eyes grow round.

She wanted to make some quip because obviously Raif couldn't mean what it sounded like.

Except Raif's expression was serious to the point of being stern. He looked magnificent and regal, so different to the man who'd made love to her in the shower an hour ago.

Tara remembered his hard body behind hers, her palms flat to the wall and his hands on her breasts as warm water sluiced down and they shattered together in waves of rapture. She'd needed Raif's support not to crumple to the floor.

So often in the last week she'd turned to Raif, depending on him. Yet now it was Raif undermining her world.

'You mean as in *wife*?'

'Wife-to-be.' He paused as if choosing his words. 'Under Nahrati law and custom you're my betrothed.'

'That's…unbelievable!'

He raised his shoulders. 'Yet it's true.'

Tara frowned, trying to fathom what was happening. 'Are you seriously trying to tell me you accept this custom? That you're meekly going to pretend we're an item because of some words you spoke in the heat of the moment?'

One of his sleek black eyebrows rose. 'We *are* an item. Or do you dispute that?' He didn't wait for her answer. 'It's not a matter of accepting, but facing facts. From the moment I called you mine everyone understood what that meant.'

'Everyone except me!' Tara wrapped her arms around her middle, holding in the waves of emotion that battered her.

'The important thing was that your kidnappers understood. That's why they gave themselves up, because they knew I'd be merciless in seeking vengeance if they abducted my woman.'

Raif's woman.

The words reverberated through her as they had two days ago. Did she feel horrified or outraged?

Or even secretly excited? Because despite her efforts not to face it, Tara was pretty sure she'd fallen in love with Raif.

She'd pretended not to notice that particular revelation, because noticing meant facing that hers was a hopeless case.

Love hadn't figured in her plans, at least for the near future, and as for marriage, surely that was a long way off. She'd told herself not to expect too much from this affair. It was just sex, for him at least, not the basis of anything long term.

Now here he was talking about her as his bride. Which would make him her husband. It was ludicrous. She wanted to laugh at the absurdity of it. Except her emotions were so jumbled she might end up in tears instead.

Still Raif refused to smile and break the tension clogging the air between them.

Tara hefted a breath, trying to find something to ground herself.

'Were you really going to take me out there without explaining?'

That was better; outrage and brewing anger were better than shock and that feeling of helplessness. She didn't allow herself to think of her sliver of delight at the news.

As if marrying Raif were really an option!

'No, of course not.'

Tara looked at the open door to the balcony. 'You left it rather late to tell me.'

She chilled to the marrow. He'd known but he hadn't told her. She felt manipulated. Duped.

Powerless in this impossible situation.

Raif reached out and tugged her arms free, took her hands in his, smoothing his thumbs over them in a soothing motion he'd used before. Then, she'd welcomed the connection between them. Now it felt like he was using his knowledge of her weaknesses against her.

Did he guess how she felt about him?

The idea stole her breath, leaving her horrified.

It was one thing to discover she'd fallen in love for the first time. In love with a man who had so little in common with her that their lives barely intersected. It was another to think he had also realised.

'I know it's a shock. I should have told you earlier,' he finally admitted ruefully. 'But I thought it would save an unnecessary argument if you saw for yourself how things stand.'

'You waited this long to avoid an argument? That's outrageous. I had a right to know.' Her voice rose.

'I agree. But if I'd told you what was happening you'd have refused to leave your suite and come here, wouldn't you?'

'Yes. No!' She shook her head, not sure what she'd have done, but suspecting he was right. 'Maybe.'

'See? I'd hoped for time to break the situation to you gradually but it's been thrust on us sooner than even I had imagined. Whether we like it or not, this is unavoidable. There was no point wasting time arguing with you over it when you can see the reality for yourself.'

He gestured to the open window through which that ponderous hum seemed louder than ever. 'That—thousands of people gathered to wish us well—is the reality.'

'That's what that sound is?' Tara swallowed, her throat scratchy.

'It is. Look.'

Raif moved to one side of the full-length windows and pulled her close. Automatically Tara inhaled that delicious scent of sandalwood, freshly laundered clothes and essence of Raif, warm and spicy. She felt that dizzying spiral of longing and the desire to lean into his big frame. Instead she peeped out at a sea of people. The streets and park, the rooftops and windows were obscured by crowds. Not only crowds but also Nahrati flags and banners featuring a golden scimitar on a scarlet background, the symbol of the royal house.

It was like something out of a movie. Unreal.

She shook her head. 'It's impossible.'

'Of course it's possible. All you have to do is step out onto the balcony. You've done it before.'

Sharply she looked up and caught the glimmer of a smile in that dark gaze.

'You think this is *funny*?' Her breathing fractured as she struggled to drag in enough oxygen.

'Of course not. But nor is it some terrible tragedy. They want to cheer you, not hurt you.'

'You can't seriously ask me to go out and pretend to be your fiancée.'

His gleam of humour vanished. 'I'm not asking you to pretend. You *are* my fiancée. Why not give the people what they want? Just the sight of you.'

Tara shook her head, grappling to understand how he could seem so sanguine. 'But it would be a lie. We're not—'

'I don't lie, Tara.' He paused, his gaze searching. 'Is it so much to ask? I've protected you. Saved you from abduction twice now. My people have stood by you even when they were threatened by armed intruders. All they want is to wish us well. Would you deny them that?'

He made it sound like all that had happened was her fault, but she was an innocent victim.

Yet it was true the townspeople had been endangered because of her. Raif had gone out of his way to keep her safe, not once but twice.

She owed him.

He didn't say it but the knowledge hung between them, weighing on her conscience.

A hundred arguments formed in Tara's head. All the reasons it was a terrible idea to go out and let those eager citizens believe in a marriage that wasn't going to happen. But Raif's words caught at her. He'd done so much for her, more than she could reasonably have expected. His people had supported her, a stranger from another land, even when they were threatened with violence.

How could she not do this when so many people were waiting for her? How long would they stay there, waiting, if she didn't show?

Tara breathed a shuddery sigh and nodded, resolving to worry about what happened next when this was done.

'Okay. But then we talk.'

Raif wasn't surprised at the roar as he led Tara onto the balcony. The story had spread of how she'd stood proudly before her attackers, offering to go with them. Of how she'd fretted for his safety as he persuaded the men to surrender and of her concern for the other women. All tipped the scales in her favour, despite the fact her family came from Dhalkur.

His people were fighters, proud of their heritage and distrustful of strangers, yet they prized gallantry and had a strong romantic streak. Tara's strength in the face of danger, and Raif's action to save her, had caught their imagination.

It seemed even the naysayers were changing their minds about her, in the face of the tide of public opinion.

In her shimmering green gown she looked radiant. A truly beautiful bride-to-be.

Raif suppressed a tight smile. He was the only one who knew her radiance owed as much to temper as excitement.

His Tara was nothing if not feisty and he expected a battle royal when they were alone together. He almost looked forward to it.

Maybe he was tired of people who wanted to agree with him. Particularly women.

Maybe he anticipated using more than compelling arguments to convince her to marry.

Whatever the reason, he smiled easily, proud as he stood beside her.

How many other women would carry this off as Tara did? He'd been right to wait till the last moment to tell her. If he'd explained earlier there'd have been arguments and attitude. This way the force of her anger was channelled somewhere useful, presenting a proud and happy face for the people of Nahrat.

Nor did she have time to wonder about how Fuad had reacted to the news. Raif remembered Fuad's voice, almost incoherent with rage over the phone, and vowed to avoid mentioning her cousin for as long as he could.

'You do this very well,' he murmured as she lifted her hand and the noise swelled.

'I haven't *done* anything,' she said through her smile. 'They'd applaud anyone who stood here with you.'

There was some truth in that, except Raif knew Tara's attitude in the desert town had won hearts. As had her charm at the couple of events she'd attended in the city. That, combined with his people's belief that he'd never choose a woman who was anything less than perfect for him and his nation, did the rest.

That was the remarkable thing. Tara was in many ways his perfect match. More suited than the contenders his aunt and royal advisers insisted on bringing to court.

'My people know I would never bring just *anyone* here.' He caught her hand and brought it to his lips, smiling as he saw her eyes catch fire. He knew that look, as he knew that tremor in her hand. 'I would only bring my future wife.'

The words resonated through him. Instead of feeling caged or caught out by this turn of events, Raif felt satisfaction.

He kissed the back of her hand then her palm, and the crowd went wild.

Raif barely noticed. He was busy watching Tara fight and fail to hide her response. The sultry, veiled look, the parted lips, the swift rise of her breasts beneath the beaded dress, and the scent of her, rich and sweet with a slight undertone of musk that betrayed arousal.

He lowered her hand and turned to face his people. 'One last wave.' Then, with cheers filling the air, he led Tara inside and closed the doors behind them. Releasing her, he strode to the door on the other side of the room and locked it.

'What are you doing?' Tara's voice was breathless and carnal excitement scudded through him. Raif knew that tone of voice, but first things first.

'Ensuring my chamberlain doesn't bustle in. You wanted to talk.'

Raif suppressed a smile as he saw her disappointment. Soon, he promised himself. He gestured to a sofa and waited for her to sit before crossing the room to sit beside her.

Tara shot him a look that confirmed she'd expected

him to sit opposite her. But they weren't strangers or enemies. She was his woman and he preferred to be beside her. Besides, he had no compunction about using their phenomenal attraction to win his case.

'Tell me what's bothering you.' He took her hand and laced her fingers with his.

'Bothering me!' She swung round to fix him with a stare. 'This whole farcical set-up!'

'Unusual, I admit, but not farcical. Believe me, this is not a situation I take lightly.'

She swallowed and nodded and he knew she fought for composure. 'Good. That's…good. Then how do you plan to get us out of this?'

Raif stroked her fingers, enjoying the way they fitted into his. 'Our betrothal will end in the usual way, with marriage.'

Tara's hand jerked and he firmed his grip. 'You've got to be kidding.'

'I'd never joke about such a thing.'

'You can't want to marry me. And I don't want to marry you.'

Raif's fingers tightened reflexively till he realised and relaxed his hold. 'Have you enjoyed being with me, Tara?'

'Of course. But that's not—'

'Relevant? It's very relevant. We have a connection that's very rare.' He paused and stroked her hand. 'With your lack of experience you may not understand how rare.'

Her brow wrinkled. 'Is that why you're going along with this? Is it tied up with some antiquated idea about having taken my virginity?'

It was true that weighed on his conscience. It was

also a source of fierce pride and excitement, knowing he was her first lover. But he was more concerned with being her last and only lover.

'I've never been with a virgin before, *habibti*, but, despite the honour of knowing you gave me your innocence, that wouldn't make me offer for your hand.'

She shook her head emphatically. 'You haven't offered. This isn't a marriage proposal. It's a stunt, a PR exercise.'

'That's what's bothering you?' Raif leaned closer, capturing her other hand where it pressed her collarbone. He kissed one then the other, inhaling her rose and cinnamon scent. 'Tara Michaels, would you do me the inestimable honour of marrying me?'

Instead of melting at his words, she stiffened. Tara shot to her feet, pulling free and stumbling towards the window before swinging to face him, eyes wounded. 'That's not funny.'

'I wasn't aiming for humour.' Raif stood, pride stiffening his spine.

'You're seriously talking about marriage?'

Did she think he made a habit of proposing? Never had Raif offered marriage. Never had he thought about spending the rest of his life with any woman, though he'd known it was his duty to marry one day to secure the throne.

'Deadly serious.'

Once more she shook her head. He reminded himself the circumstances were extraordinary.

'Why should I marry you? I barely know you.'

Raif's patience splintered. He'd been prepared for arguments and doubts but not that tone of disdain, as if she didn't care for him at all. As if his offer wasn't worthy of consideration.

His hands clenched at his sides as he drew himself up. He thought of all those beautiful, talented, amenable women who'd come to his court, vying for his attention and a chance to become Sheikha of Nahrat. He'd been attracted to some, but not enough to contemplate marriage. Now, when circumstance forced his hand, his honourable offer was spurned.

'You think I'd planned to marry a woman brought to me by a rug seller? A woman whose entry to court was in a rolled-up carpet?'

There. That proved it. The scorn in his voice showed how little he wanted this match.

Tara should be grateful the truth had won out. Instead she felt a hot ball of misery form in the pit of her stomach. Her mouth crumpled and she had to work to face that derisive stare.

'One of the reasons I've been so diplomatically successful in the region is that I'm single,' Raif said after a lengthy silence. His flash of anger had disappeared. 'Several nations hold hopes of closer ties with Nahrat through a royal marriage.'

Had he a *tendre* for some other woman? The idea tore at her. She knew so little about Raif.

Except that, despite the hurt and dismay, part of her wanted to say *yes* to his proposal, as if marrying a man she'd known less than two weeks was a sane move. As if he hadn't cornered her into this.

'So this engagement…' the word was bitter on Tara's tongue '…would scupper that.'

Raif inclined his head. 'It would. But there are other benefits.'

Tara blinked. How could he look at her with familiar warmth in his eyes when a moment ago he'd scorned her?

'Name one. Apart from the fact that your people expect it, and that we're sexually compatible.'

His eyebrows rose as his voice dropped to a decadently low rumble. 'More than compatible, Tara. What we have is unique.'

'Marriage is about more than sex.'

'I agree. It's about constancy, support, respect, patience. Being a partner. I believe we can be all those things to each other.'

That surprised her. He spoke as if he really understood what made a successful marriage. His words evoked memories of her parents, who'd been so happy together.

'You look surprised. But I have the example of my parents. They were very happily married.'

'It was a love match?'

Dark eyes held hers, his look compelling. Tara had the uncomfortable feeling Raif read the thoughts behind her question and silently cursed herself for asking.

'It was an arranged match, in line with family tradition, but there was respect and affection.' He paused. 'Is that why you're hesitant? Because you want a declaration of love?'

'No!' Her voice was strident, almost blotting out his words. Her skin crawled at the idea Raif read her feelings. 'But marriage between two strangers is doomed to fail.'

Even if another Tara, one deep inside, thought marrying Raif was the best idea she'd ever heard.

'You will have my respect and support, Tara. I will help you every step of the way.' His brows drew together in a hint of a frown. 'It's true I'm used to getting my own way, but I promise to work on sharing, on negotiating. You won't find me unreasonable.'

From a man who'd spent years as the ultimate power in Nahrat that was an amazing concession. Did he realise her frozen horror at the idea of having no control in her own life? Her heart beat faster.

'I promise to be faithful too. There will be no other women.' The way he spoke, his gaze holding hers, his voice low and deep, made her shiver with something like excitement. 'And I expect faithfulness from you.'

That was no problem. Tara suspected that after being with Raif, no other man could compete.

Then she realised where her thoughts were heading and pulled back. 'You still haven't told me what you'd get out of this. Apart from good sex and avoiding a scandal. Surely marrying a woman brought to the palace *by a carpet seller* is beneath your dignity.' Her heart pounded as she recalled Raif's contempt.

'Forgive me, Tara. That comment was uncalled for.' Raif spread his hands, his apology taking her by surprise. 'You bruised my pride, saying you didn't want to marry me.'

That wasn't what she'd said. The idea of marrying him was far too tempting.

'We're well suited, you know. Both determined and proud. Both questioning. Both…attracted.' He paused. 'I'd acquire a wife with warmth and people skills that will be beneficial in a royal bride. You're royal too, though you don't admit it. And, despite negativity from those who object to me taking a Dhalkuri wife, tying our nations is good for peace.' His lips twitched in a smile that tugged at her heart. 'Plus, I'd be marrying an heiress.'

Tara thought of his reaction when she'd accused him of wanting her inheritance. He clearly had no need for her money. She ignored his joke. 'There are people who object to the betrothal?'

He shrugged. 'Some still see Dhalkur as the old enemy. I hope to change that. Our marriage would bring us closer to long-term peace.'

Tara stared at Raif. His expression was reasonable, his stance open. Yet she couldn't believe his fatalistic acceptance of the situation, as if he had no choice.

This was a man who made his own fate. The way he'd faced down her abductors, strolling in despite their weapons, proved that. Something else was going on here. She just didn't know what.

Tara thought back to how he'd held her arm, not just in the desert town, but here in the palace, when he led her to dinner. Had he been staking a claim then? If so, why?

'You don't need to say yes straight away, Tara.' Suddenly he was right before her, so close she had to lift her chin to meet his eyes. 'I know this is a shock and you need time to get used to the idea.'

A warm arm wrapped around her waist, tugging her close. He was all muscle and hard bone, and everything inside her melted. Tara fought to keep her mind focused on their conversation, but her body remembered the ecstasy they'd shared.

'Let me help you get used to the idea,' he murmured as he kissed her neck, sending shivers of delight through her.

'I…'

Raif's mouth brushed the corner of hers as he lifted her high against his solid chest. Tara tried to gather her thoughts and her resistance. She needed to think this through, but as he lowered her to a wide sofa and joined her there, it was impossible. Nothing mattered but the magic Raif wrought on her eager body. She'd have to think later.

CHAPTER FOURTEEN

TWO DAYS LATER, the news came that Tara's uncle was dead. Raif broke it to her and she was glad of his presence. The way he held her close in his arms, not talking, just offering the comfort of his embrace, was pure solace.

The death had been expected—and she hadn't been close to her uncle—but it felt as if the final family link to her mother died with him. Her uncle had known her mother well and had been able to reminisce with Tara about her. That had been precious.

'You'll be okay,' Raif murmured, not asking, but reminding her.

'I know.' Yet she didn't break his hold.

Theirs was a crazy relationship. Though they lived together and slept together, Tara had refused to accompany Raif to any public events since they'd appeared before his people.

She sensed his impatience, but to her it felt like a lie, letting everyone believe they were to marry.

Even though Raif seemed convinced they would.

No matter what argument she made, he'd reiterate that actions had consequences, that they needed to face their situation and make the most of it. He talked of respect and admiration, companionship and caring, and Tara slid further under his spell, despite her attempts to be clear-headed.

When Raif was near it was hard to imagine life without him. His personality was bigger than life-size. He had such presence that around him she felt energised in a way that made her old life seem humdrum and stale.

And because she loved him.

Now, alone in her suite a day later, she faced that truth.

Did she really want to return to grey London and work selling gems for other people to wear? Did she want to turn her back on this man who, infuriating and challenging as he could be, made her feel stronger and more alive? With Raif she even felt cherished. She told herself it was an illusion, that he was making the best of their situation, yet it felt real, and her vulnerable heart responded wholeheartedly.

If she wasn't careful one day soon she'd give in and agree to marry him.

The thought sent her to her feet. She'd been stuck inside too long. She needed to get out and think.

Raif had flown out early to pay his respects at her uncle's funeral, which traditionally was a male-only affair, and attend the new Sheikh's coronation.

The thought of Fuad made her more restless than ever.

She left her apartment and made for the palace's main entrance. With the funeral and coronation today she'd be safe to venture out. Fuad would have no interest in her once he was crowned and Tara was desperate to get away from the palace.

Maybe she'd visit the spice markets and lose herself in the sights, sounds and smells. Or visit a park or explore the streets of the old city.

She'd reached the grand vestibule when a man stopped before her. He bowed. 'Ms Michaels. I'm afraid I can't let you pass.'

'Sorry?' She stared, recognising him as one of Raif's security staff. 'I'm just going for a walk.'

She spread her hands in an open gesture. She didn't even have a purse. A reminder that everything she had here she owed to Raif's largesse.

'Even so.' His voice was apologetic but his solid form barred her way. 'His Majesty asked that you remain in the palace.'

Asked? He hadn't asked. He'd ordered.

Just like Fuad.

Shock was an iron clamp across her shoulders and neck. It weighted her lungs, making it hard to breathe.

Tara blinked and turned away, making for the other side of the vestibule, only to have another guard step from the shadows.

She slammed to a stop, the hairs at her nape rising. This was ridiculous! She was safe from Fuad now. There was no reason for Raif to keep her here.

She looked out to the warm sunlight, the bustling city she'd never really explored.

Her heart beat faster. She could make a run for it. But the guards would catch her before she got far. She stood, fuming, the feeling of isolation growing. She hadn't minded when Raif was here but now it struck her like a blow.

'Good morning, Ms Michaels.' It was the chamberlain, smiling as he crossed the vestibule. 'Please, come inside and let me see to whatever you require.'

'I want to go out.'

His smile slipped. 'I'm afraid that's not possible until His Majesty returns later today. Please.' He put his arm out, ushering her back inside.

For a moment she wavered, wondering if they'd use force if she stalked outside. Then common sense stopped her. She'd embarrass them and herself.

Her argument was with Raif. What was he thinking, to lock her up when there was no need? Didn't he understand she'd spent too long locked away? This was too much like being Fuad's prisoner. Though Raif tried to protect her it felt like control, and that chafed. More so now when she felt trapped by his marriage plans.

Reluctantly she accompanied the chamberlain.

'Thank you, Ms Michaels. Now, if there's something I can get you?'

'Nothing, thank you.' She was tired of being alone but she didn't have the patience for polite conversation with Raif's man. She wanted to make her own decisions, not feel her every move was being managed. She didn't even have her work in the treasury to distract her as her colleague was out of the city visiting family.

Tara drew a slow breath. Who would she visit if she had the chance? Not the remnants of her family. There were friends in London but no one particularly close. The realisation intensified that sharp pang of loneliness. It wasn't long since she'd lost her mother.

'You'll have company tomorrow,' the chamberlain said. 'His Majesty's aunt is returning. She's eager to meet you.'

Tara didn't doubt it. His aunt was probably hurrying home to check out how unsuitable Raif's bride-to-be was. Had he told her how Tara had arrived in the palace, and how he'd been forced into naming her as his to save her life?

She shivered. Was she supposed to wait here meekly, to be inspected like some broodmare prior to purchase?

That was unfair, she knew it was. But this, today, was the last straw.

For weeks she'd felt trapped, unable to make the slightest decisions for herself. Even falling in love, at times glorious and exciting, was tainted with the knowledge Raif didn't return her feelings. He wanted to marry because it was expected. Even so, she suspected there was something he wasn't telling her. Another reason behind his insistence.

Maybe he did want access to the mineral wealth she'd inherited after all. Or maybe relations with Dhalkur were worse than she'd imagined and marriage would stop a complete rift between the countries.

Whatever his thinking, he didn't love her. The chances were he never would. If she stayed she'd be trapped, not just by people's expectations but by her yearning heart.

A trembling started in her knees, a sick feeling in her stomach. She remembered being truly helpless as a teenager when choice had been stripped from her by a guy who intended to take rather than ask.

Raif wasn't like him. Raif protected her.

Yet he kept making decisions for her.

Could she live here, loving Raif, but never having the freedom to express it, or the freedom to make her own choices?

'Ms Michaels?'

The chamberlain was frowning at her.

'Sorry. My mind was elsewhere. Please excuse me.'

It was late when Raif returned. His steps quickened as he thought of Tara waiting for him, and the news he had for her. He imagined her bright smile, her relief, the way she'd sink into his arms—

'Tara?' What was she doing here, on a chair outside his study? 'Are you okay? I was coming to your suite.'

She stood and he saw she wore the raspberry-red dress she'd had on the day he first saw her. His lips twitched in appreciation. She looked alluring whatever she wore but he had a particular fondness for that simple dress, especially given how easily it opened.

'We need to talk.' Instead of turning to walk with him, she opened his study door and stepped in.

Raif halted, puzzled. Where was her welcome smile? Why talk in his study instead of in her suite, where there was a comfortable bed?

He followed, closing the door.

'How did today go?' She stood on the far side of his desk and for the first time in ages didn't meet his eyes.

Something wasn't right. He felt it in his bones.

'Your uncle was farewelled with appropriate honours.' He paused. 'And the coronation took place, but not as most people expected.'

'What happened?' *Now* she met his gaze.

'The royal council voted in favour of Salim rather than Fuad. The only person surprised was Fuad.'

'You mean Salim is Sheikh? That's wonderful!' Tara shook her head. 'What part did you play in all this?'

'Me? It was the Council who chose the Sheikh.' All Raif had done was ensure Salim got into the country despite his brother's attempts to keep him out. And speak privately with some of the country's powerbrokers about what a future would look like under Fuad's rule.

'Whatever it was you did, thank you. That's a marvellous outcome.'

Raif heard the warmth in her tone and crossed to her, only to see her stiffen and step back. He froze, reading her tense body language.

'What's happened?' He'd been sure she'd be safe from Fuad's machinations here, but desperate men did desperate things. 'Did someone try something?' His heart stilled on the thought.

'No one had a chance, since I wasn't allowed out.' The mutinous twist of her lips betrayed her thoughts.

That was the reason for her distance?

'It was a precaution. I couldn't trust Fuad not to try to grab you at the last moment.'

'He thought he was going to be made Sheikh. He wasn't thinking about me today. Besides, if you thought that way you should have discussed it with me.' The clipped way she enunciated each word made it clear she wasn't pleased.

'Would you have been happier if you'd gone out and his men abducted you?'

She folded her arms under her breasts and he fought to keep his attention on her face, not her cleavage. 'I'd have been happier if you'd talked to me instead of making decisions for me.'

Raif spread his hands. 'It was for the best.' He paused then admitted, 'I don't want anything happening to you.'

For a second it looked like she understood. He read

warmth and longing in her glittering eyes and an answering heat filled his chest.

'You made me a prisoner.'

'Sorry?'

'You locked me up so I wasn't *allowed* to go out.'

'I explained—'

'I spent a week as Fuad's prisoner and then, from the moment I arrived here, you dictated what I could do and where I could go.'

Raif shook his head. 'I don't recall that stopping you. Who was it who announced her presence to the world by slipping out onto the royal balcony?'

'That was one mistake.'

'You haven't been a prisoner. You've been an honoured guest.'

She'd been received with all hospitality. Had she no concept of what he'd done for her? The rules he'd broken, the backlash he'd faced to keep her safe? Hadn't he lavished care and affection on her? Hadn't he shared himself in ways he never had with any other woman? He'd offered her marriage!

'I haven't once ventured out of here except with you. Not once!'

Her contrariness annoyed him. 'Now you blame me for protecting you from Fuad?'

'You're deliberately misunderstanding.' Her chin hiked high and this time Raif found it infuriating rather than attractive.

'What, exactly, is your problem, princess?' He realised his mistake as he drawled the last word and glimpsed hurt behind her anger. He stepped nearer. 'Tara, I—'

'My problem is that from the day I arrived you've

told me what to do. You've made every decision. You've given me no choice. I'm not even allowed to go for a walk in the city without your approval. I have no *freedom*. You're trying to railroad me into believing we have to marry because you called me your woman when you saved me.'

At least she acknowledged he'd saved her!

Raif stood taller, feeling her words like a smack to his pride. He'd done everything he could for her. More than anyone could reasonably expect.

'This is the thanks I get?'

'See? I question you and you stare down that superior nose of yours as if I shouldn't even dare to speak.'

'You're twisting this out of proportion.'

Tara jammed her hands onto her hips. 'No, I'm telling you what it's like from where I stand.'

Again Raif saw pain in her eyes and the crumpled corners of her lovely mouth. He was torn between wanting to haul her into his arms and wanting to put her in her place.

Except her place was a moot point. He'd told himself at first she was simply someone who needed his help. Then she'd become his lover and life got much more complicated. Claiming her as his betrothed should have simplified things yet it all felt tangled. His reasoning, his feelings, and certainly her responses.

Raif was used to making considered decisions and implementing them. He was used to knowing he did the best for his people. Most times he was right.

Tara robbed him of that certainty. She made him feel…

That was the problem. She made him *feel*.

'From where I'm standing there's something fishy

about this. There's something you're not telling me. I can't believe you'd marry a complete stranger just because you called her your woman. All it would take is a few words from you to correct the situation.'

Raif's belly clamped and he felt an unfamiliar surge of panic skitter through him. 'Are you calling me a liar?'

'I'm saying things aren't as black and white as you make out.' She breathed deep then said in a rush, 'I want to leave. If you'll lend me the money I'll go to London tomorrow, or tonight if there's a flight.'

He couldn't be hearing this. It felt like everything had turned to slow motion. 'Lend you money?'

'I'm good for it. I've got money in the bank and I'm an heiress, remember?' She shot him a haughty look that chilled his blood. Where was his warm, welcoming Tara? 'Or are you going to say that passport you promised isn't ready? Which reminds me, you didn't return my driving licence. Are you withholding them to keep me imprisoned here?'

Never in his life had Raif felt such incandescent rage.

On top of everything else she doubted his word. He'd done everything for her. He'd planned to give her even more. His thoughts skidded to a halt, shying away from that. He stalked to his desk and yanked open a drawer.

'Here.' He slapped the temporary diplomatic passport onto his desk with her licence. 'I was going to give it to you tomorrow.' After he persuaded her into an early wedding.

Raif had the satisfaction of seeing her mouth drop open, but her surprise only inflamed his temper. No one ever had insulted him so. Tara had turned what should have been triumph into bitter dispute and sour disappointment.

Disappointment? It felt like more than that, but Raif had no intention of examining his feelings in front of her.

It infuriated him that she had the power to undo him. To fog his brain and destroy his peace and make him feel...appalling. Bruised pride urged him to let her leave, but something stronger made him try one more time.

'What will you do with your precious *freedom*, Tara? Go back to work in a jewellery store? Is that the summit of your ambition? Do you know your mentor from the museum approached me? He's so impressed he wants you to undertake formal studies then work for him long-term.'

Was that a flare of interest in her narrowed eyes? But just as he thought he'd got through to her, Tara's expression turned blank. Where was the enthusiastic, fascinating woman he knew? Why was she hiding? Raif didn't believe this was about her being kept inside today.

'Not interested?' He waited for her counter-attack and got none. His heart sank. 'Why, Tara? Because you're too scared to think bigger? You'd rather live a boring life that doesn't fulfil you than take a risk? Is that why you deny your royal position, because you don't think you can live up to it?' The words spilled from Raif in a furious rush. 'Is that why you reject *me*?'

'I don't want to argue, Raif. I want to leave.'

Everything about her, from her stiff shoulders to her flat stare, told him she'd shut him out. He wanted to rage and force her to argue. He wanted to hold her close and persuade her to yield. But he had his pride.

'If you're so eager to escape this *prison*,' his lips curled on the word, 'I'll arrange a flight tonight.'

Raif waited, daring her to agree. She wouldn't, he knew. Despite her accusations, she cared for him. He felt it in her tenderness, her eager smiles. When she thought about it, she'd—

'Perfect.' Her eyes flashed as she stepped up and swiped the pieces of identification off his desk.

She didn't mean it. She was bluffing. In a second she'd see her error and apologise.

'I don't have anything to pack, so I'm ready to leave as soon as a flight's ready. I'll wait in my room till then.'

To Raif's amazement she swung towards the door.

'Wait!'

She turned back. Was that hope in her eyes? No, it was a trick of the light. She was as ungrateful and obstinate as before.

He reached into the drawer and pulled out a velvet box. He'd intended to give it to her as an engagement gift, until she'd thrown his generosity in his teeth and made a mockery of everything he'd done for her.

'A going-away present.' Raif didn't push it across the table but tossed it. She caught it but didn't even look at it.

'Thank you for your hospitality, Raif.'

Then she was gone in a flounce of crimson cotton.

CHAPTER FIFTEEN

TARA SHOVED HER hands in her pockets and scuffed the fallen leaves with her boot. The London park was damp from autumn drizzle, perfectly matching her mood.

She'd made the biggest mistake of her life.

Leaving Raif should have been the most sensible decision.

She couldn't marry a man who didn't love her. Or who made every important decision. It would be disastrous. She'd felt herself falling more in love while Raif remained self-contained.

Tara didn't want self-contained. She wanted love as well as passion, partnership not bossiness.

She wanted to be an equal, not a subject to be ordered about.

Yet there was no doubt, she shouldn't have stormed off in a temper. She should have stayed and got to the bottom of Raif's behaviour. Talked with him, negotiated, listened, pried, whatever it took to get beyond his demands and obstinate pride and discover why he insisted on marriage.

She'd achieved nothing by leaving except to sever their connection and make herself utterly miserable.

Tara had spent the last week packing up and arranging for the sale of her mother's home. She'd returned to work only to give notice. Raif had been right. Much as she'd loved that job she'd feel stultified returning there.

She kicked more leaves, watching the flurry of brown and gold, and saw two women across the park staring. Were they going to tell her to get back on the path?

Footsteps crunched on gravel behind her and she realised they weren't looking at her. They were gaping at—

'Tara.'

She swung round so fast she almost toppled.

Her throat seized up even as her heart accelerated.

'Raif!' He looked different. Magnificent but unfamiliar. It wasn't merely the cashmere coat over his open-necked shirt. Unfamiliar lines bracketed his mouth and his eyes looked tired. 'What are you doing in London?'

'I had business to conclude.'

Tara's heart dived towards her toes. For a moment she'd thought he'd come for her. After what she'd said to him it was a wonder he even spoke to her.

'I'm sorry for what I said.' She met his stare. 'I was ungrateful. I know you weren't keeping me prisoner. I—'

'You were under considerable stress. You'd lost your mother then your uncle. You'd been physically threatened and you'd just begun your first sexual relationship. Naturally you were emotional. You felt powerless.'

Her mouth turned down. Her first sexual relationship? It had been much more to her. She didn't want a relationship with any man but Raif. Her throat was so tight it hurt to swallow.

'You're very understanding.'

His shoulders lifted. 'When I'm not in a temper.' Was that a curl of humour teasing his mouth? No, she imagined it.

'Why are you here?' Her sweeping hand encompassed the bare trees and dog walkers.

'I followed you from the house.'

Tara's breath hissed in. 'Sorry?'

'I saw you walking towards the park when I drove up.'

Why would Raif want to see her after all she'd said?

'I'm not pregnant.' Her period had begun the day after she arrived in England. No doubt hormones had played a part in her distress that last day in Nahrat.

His eyes widened. 'I see.'

Tara stood waiting, but he said nothing more. Maybe he hadn't come to check on possible consequences from their affair? Something tingled inside her.

'Have you heard from Salim?'

She frowned. He wanted to talk about her cousin? 'No. Is he all right?'

'He's fine. But Fuad is dead.' Tara gasped and he continued. 'Straight after the coronation he got in his sports car and headed out of the capital. Witnesses say he was in a furious temper, and the experts say he was doing double the speed limit when he failed to take a curve and crashed.'

Tara hadn't had the energy to follow news reports since leaving Nahrat. But she could imagine Fuad in a fit of pique, flinging out of the palace and taking out his temper in reckless driving. He'd been so obsessed with winning the throne.

'So he won't bother you again.'

That was why he'd come. She met Raif's steely gaze and that little tremor of excitement that he'd come because he'd missed her died.

'I see. Thank you for coming to tell me.'

'That's not all.'

She tilted her head in enquiry. She didn't really want to hear what else Fuad had done. It was too hard standing here, so close to Raif, seeing him look so distant. She thought of the hope she'd harboured, the action she'd planned, and knew they were futile.

'You were right when you said there was something suspicious about my actions. That I wouldn't let myself be forced into marriage.'

Tara blinked and stumbled back a step, shocked by the change of subject.

'What are you saying, Raif?'

He closed the gap between them, filling her vision. She inhaled sharply, dragging in the smell of warm flesh, brisk autumn air and a hint of sandalwood. Her pulse thrummed faster and she dug her fists deeper in her pockets so as not to reach for him.

'I used that as an excuse because I didn't want to let you go.' He paused as if watching for a response. She was too stunned to give one.

'I told myself it was fate but I was simply using whatever reason I could find to keep you close. Looking back, I know I was only too ready to flout the rules where you were concerned, touching you in public at that palace dinner and on other visits. As if I wanted the world to know you were mine, though I didn't fully acknowledge the implications.'

Tara fought for calm as excitement vied with disbelief. She breathed deeply, trying to think logically.

'You mean you didn't think about how others would interpret it?'

He shook his head slowly, his lips curving up in a slow smile that stole the air from her lungs.

'I mean I didn't face what it meant about *my* feelings. I wanted you, Tara. But it wasn't all about sex. I've never felt like this with any other lover. I want you in every way a man can want a woman. *That's* why I want you to marry me. You make me feel complete in ways I'd never imagined. It's a new and scary experience, discovering I'm not the loner I believed myself to be. Finding out a small, feisty stranger has the power to undo me.'

His smile faded and to her amazement Tara heard his breathing turn ragged. She replayed his words, unable to believe what she thought she'd heard.

She felt dazed, as if he'd tipped the world upside down and nothing made sense.

'You still want to marry me?' Her voice shook.

'That's why I'm here. Nothing's right since you left. My staff avoid me because I'm in a perennial bad mood and my aunt thinks I'm pining.'

Suddenly it felt like the sun broke free of the louring clouds, warming her chilled flesh. She told herself it couldn't be true, yet she couldn't prevent hope unfurling.

'Because of me?'

He nodded. 'I care for you, Tara. I care deeply. I

know you'll say it's too soon, that we haven't known each other long enough, but—'

'I wouldn't.'

Hadn't her parents fallen for each other at first sight?

Tara swallowed hard and gathered her nerve, taking heart from the emotions she saw in Raif's tense features.

'I feel the same. You were right about my old life not fitting any more. I want so much more. I'm booked on a flight to Nahrat today.'

His hand shot out, closing around her elbow, and she was grateful for his touch as her knees wobbled.

'To see me?'

She nodded, stunned to read in Raif's proud features the same desperate hope she felt.

Suddenly what had seemed impossibly risky became urgent. Shattered hopes reassembled, banishing the shadows of hurt and fear.

'Yes.' Tara had to draw another breath to steady herself. 'Because I love you.'

How easy it was to say the words, after all that soul-searching. But Raif had confounded her fears and doubts.

Powerful arms wrapped round her, pulling her against his chest. Soft cashmere enfolded her and beneath her ear she felt the chaotic pound of his heart. She'd never heard anything so wonderful.

Raif's lips pressed to her hair and then her upturned face.

'That's my line.' He sounded breathless, like a man who'd run for his life. 'I love you, Tara. I don't have the words to tell you how much.'

But his expression told her. And his thudding heart and shaking hands.

'I believed that love would make me weak, which is why I fought it, fought *you*. But this doesn't feel like weakness, *habibti*. It feels right.' Raif drew in a deep breath. 'I have a lot to learn about sharing and not being so autocratic, but I'm determined to make you happy. I'll do whatever it takes, if you'll give me the chance.'

Her heart swelled till she thought she might burst with tenderness and excitement. She lifted her hand to cup his jaw, revelling in the feel of his skin against hers. It had been too long.

'You're wearing the bangle.' He caught her arm and held it out, where the weak sunlight caught the intricate gold work and rich red spinels.

Tara nodded. 'I didn't open the box till I was on the plane here. And when I saw what you gave me, I wondered.' Strangely she felt suddenly shy.

'You wondered why I chose that piece?'

'It's not as eye-catching as some other things in the treasury. It wasn't the obvious choice if you wanted to declare publicly that I was your bride. Since you had it handy when I insisted on leaving, I assumed that's why you had it ready to give me.'

Tara had been torn between hoping that was true and telling herself she was spinning tales out of nothing because she wanted so desperately to believe he cared.

Raif's expression made her heart roll over, 'I chose it because it moved you. You see its intrinsic beauty, the work and dedication, not just bright colour and a dollar value. I wanted you to have something that proved I see *you*, as a woman apart. A woman with her own ideas and preferences. It's not a traditional betrothal gift but it seemed perfect for the woman I want to spend the rest of my days with.'

Tara's throat worked, emotion threatening to undo her. 'Just the days?'

He swept her closer, lifted her off her feet till her face was level with his. 'And all the nights too, *habibti*. If you'll have me.'

Her eyes misted with emotion. She had the strongest feeling she didn't deserve such happiness after the way she'd deserted him, but she wasn't foolish enough to hesitate. Raif was everything to her. Her present and her future, the man who had her heart.

'How can I resist, my darling?' Tara lifted her mouth to his and let Raif sweep her up into their own private paradise.

EPILOGUE

'YOU LOOK WONDERFUL, my dear. A truly radiant bride.'
Raif's aunt straightened Tara's train then gave her a hug.

Tara hugged her back. In the last seven months she'd
grown fond of this woman whose incisive wit hid a
kind heart. She was a wonderful mentor, helping Raif
fill any gaps in Tara's knowledge about Nahrat and
the royal court.

'Thank you. The colour helps.' Tara gestured to the
cranberry satin, richly embroidered with gold, that
matched her antique bracelet, chandelier earrings and
the delicate tiara Raif had had made especially for her.

'Nonsense. It's the glow of a woman in love. My
nephew is an incredibly lucky man. Fortunately, he
has the good sense to realise it.' She smiled. 'If anyone
had told me he'd wait a whole seven months to marry
when every time he looks at you he eats you up with
his eyes…' Her smile turned mischievous. 'You're good
for him, my dear.'

Tara shook her head. 'He was the one who wanted
a long engagement.'

Raif had put her needs first. He was adamant she
needed time to adjust to life in Nahrat, find her feet
and make decisions about the wedding.

He didn't want her to feel pushed into marriage too fast. Her accusations about being a prisoner had stung his conscience and though she assured him that was in the past, he'd insisted they wait. He'd made her feel totally treasured. She'd even found time to begin her new studies, intending to fit part-time work in with her royal duties.

Salim entered the room, wearing a grin on his handsome face. 'Are you ready, cousin? Your groom is getting impatient. If I didn't know better I'd think him nervous.'

Raif's aunt laughed. 'Nonsense. It does a man good to wait for his bride.' After kissing Tara on the cheek and twitching Salim's jacket straight, she bustled out.

Salim looked Tara over. 'I'd ask if you're sure you want to marry a Nahrati but your face tells me you are. Besides, Raif's a good man.'

'I know.' Tara smiled as he hooked her arm through his. During their engagement Raif had proved his love again and again. In thoughtfulness and tenderness, but also in his willingness to listen and be swayed by her. There were still times when they disagreed but always they managed to come to some compromise. And negotiating could be such fun!

'You look like the cat who got the cream,' Salim said as he led her to the door. 'I almost feel sorry for Raif.' Tara lightly punched his arm. 'But only a little. I feel he's getting his just deserts.'

The music began, a royal fanfare that once would have made her nervous about being in the limelight. Now, as Salim led her down the red-carpeted aisle, past hundreds of guests, she felt only elation.

For there, ahead, was Raif, resplendent in gold and

white, tall and compelling. His eyes were fixed on her with a look that sealed the air in her lungs.

If ever she'd wondered what love looked like, it was this. Those ebony eyes locked on hers with such intensity she barely registered the crowd, or her cousin as he kissed her cheek and moved aside.

There was just her and Raif, the man she loved. Emotion swamped her, suddenly overwhelming. Then Raif took her hand, his strength flowing into her.

'Ready, my love?'

'Absolutely.'

Then before international royalty and a television audience of millions, Raif swept her into his arms and kissed her deeply, thoroughly and with total disregard for royal protocol.

Tara kissed him right back, her hands clamping his shoulders as she held him close. This last week, when she'd stayed at her cousin's palace, she'd missed Raif terribly. It felt an eternity since they were together.

When Raif finally lifted his head the emotion in his midnight gaze told her all she needed to know.

'I love you, Tara. I always will.'

'And I love you, Raif, for ever.' Her voice wobbled from sheer happiness.

Later they discovered that kiss had made headlines. People around the world sighed over their fairy-tale romance. It was a romance the public would follow through the years as the Sheikh and his Sheikha grew closer and their family expanded.

They created a family tradition of love at first sight and happy-ever-afters.

* * * * *

WE HOPE YOU ENJOYED
THIS BOOK FROM
HARLEQUIN
PRESENTS

Escape to exotic locations where passion knows no bounds.

Welcome to the glamorous lives of royals and billionaires, where passion knows no bounds. Be swept into a world of luxury, wealth and exotic locations.

8 NEW BOOKS AVAILABLE EVERY MONTH!

#3901 BRIDE BEHIND THE DESERT VEIL
The Marchetti Dynasty
by Abby Green

After surrendering to passion with a mystery woman, Sharif Marchetti must erase their desert encounter from his memory. Until they meet again...as he lifts the veil of his convenient wife!

#3902 THE ITALIAN'S FORBIDDEN VIRGIN
Those Notorious Romanos
by Carol Marinelli

Italian tycoon Gian de Luca knows Ariana Romano is off-limits. She's his mentor's daughter, and her drama queen reputation precedes her. But when he offers her comfort one night, he's shocked to discover she's a virgin. Perhaps he's been wrong about her all along...

#3903 HIS STOLEN INNOCENT'S VOW
The Queen's Guard
by Marcella Bell

For billionaire Drake Andros, only marriage and an heir from Helene d'Tierrza will recover what was stolen from him. Their chemistry may persuade her to help him, but her vow of innocence may complicate his plan...

#3904 ONE HOT NEW YORK NIGHT
Wanted: A Billionaire
by Melanie Milburne

A sizzling night of passion is exactly what Zoey Brackenfield needs. And since it's with Finn O'Connell, business rival and notorious playboy, there's zero chance of heartbreak. That is, until she starts craving his exhilarating touch...

YOU CAN FIND MORE INFORMATION ON UPCOMING HARLEQUIN TITLES, FREE EXCERPTS AND MORE AT HARLEQUIN.COM.

HPCNMRB0321

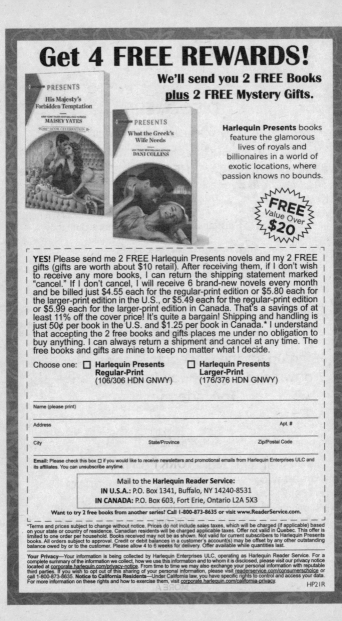

Love Harlequin romance?

DISCOVER.

Be the first to find out about promotions, news and exclusive content!

Facebook.com/HarlequinBooks

Twitter.com/HarlequinBooks

Instagram.com/HarlequinBooks

Pinterest.com/HarlequinBooks

YouTube.com/HarlequinBooks

ReaderService.com

EXPLORE.

Sign up for the Harlequin e-newsletter and download a free book from any series at
TryHarlequin.com

CONNECT.

Join our Harlequin community to share your thoughts and connect with other romance readers!
Facebook.com/groups/HarlequinConnection

HSOCIAL2021